*the*
# SPIRIT
*of*
## Nora

# the
# SPIRIT
## of
# Nora

*a novel*

LYLE SCOTT LEE

TATE PUBLISHING
AND ENTERPRISES, LLC

Published by Tate Publishing & Enterprises, LLC
127 E. Trade Center Terrace | Mustang, Oklahoma 73064 USA
1.888.361.9473 | www.tatepublishing.com

Tate Publishing is committed to excellence in the publishing industry. The company reflects the philosophy established by the founders, based on Psalm 68:11,
*"The Lord gave the word and great was the company of those who published it."*

Book design copyright © 2011 by Tate Publishing, LLC. All rights reserved.
*Cover design by Amber Gulilat*
*Interior design by Christina Hicks*

Published in the United States of America

ISBN: 978-1-61346-589-9
Fiction / Christian / Historical
11.08.31

In memory of
Nora Emelia Anderson
US Army Nurse, WWI, France
Jan 15, 1881–Jan 16, 1919

# *Prologue*

*Summer 1921*

Mrs. Nels Thorsen lifts the painting high on to the wall while her young visitor reaches behind to secure the cord over the hook. The elderly woman pushes a corner of the painting, sliding it until it is straight. Then the two women step back.

"Do you now see the similarities I spoke of?"

"Yes, I do. But *they* could be sisters as well."

"Yes. Many have said so."

The young woman slowly sits on the bed while thinking about the girl who slept here so long ago, and sleepovers, no doubt, and what secrets and dreams must have been exchanged.

"Here." Mrs. Thorsen hands her guest a note. "This accompanied the painting."

The young woman moves to stand beneath the high-noon summer light shining through the bedroom window and begins to read.

> *Dear parents of Nora Thorsen,*
> *As I write you regarding your daughter, I hope this letter finds you both well. As you may well know, she and I spent time together in Paris some years ago, as well as in the countryside of my homeland of France during the*

*war. I have always thought your daughter to be both vivacious and headstrong. And as you can see from the portrait I created of her and her dear friend Ella—while still very much in their youths—the two of them provide a luminous and inseparable bond.*

*Understandably, Nora found it difficult to look upon this painting and asked that I store it away. I sincerely believe she shall return to America someday, and I think it best that this painting should be available for her reconsideration.*

*I am certain I shall never see her again in this world, so please assure her that I return this to her with only the best of intentions.*

*Sincere regards,*

"I can't make out the author's name." The young woman walks over to the newly hung painting. "Nor can I make out the signature on the painting." Her Canadian accent is now more doleful than the aged water stain meandering down the corner wall.

"I'm sorry, but I don't recall his name, as it was so many years ago." The elderly woman feigns cheeriness. "He is a scribbler. Perhaps he wished to remain anonymous."

"To be deliberately unknown would be a luxury." The room swirls in *what ifs* and *how comes*.

"The past is in the past, dear." Mrs. Thorsen smiles as she tries to hold the young woman's thoughts in the present.

"And you *are* expecting her soon?"

"Any day now."

"Very well. She'll recall the artist's name."

"Of course."

"Maybe he can tell me things as well."

"If he can be found. As he stated, he might no longer be alive."

"I have so many … so many questions."

# The Wind Blows Wherever It Pleases

The wind blows wherever it pleases. You hear
its sound, but you cannot tell where it comes
from or where it is going. So it is with everyone born of the Spirit.

John 3:8

*June 1899*

"Bye-bye, Minnesota!" I shout as Ella and I wave from
the train window to the westerly side of the Saint
Croix River flowing wide beneath the tracks below.
Just then, the wind changes direction, blowing engine
smoke into our faces, forcing Ella to quickly shut the
window.

We both laugh, coughing, embarrassed by our
schoolgirl silliness. An elderly, portly businessman sitting up a row on the opposite side of the aisle slowly
shakes his head while working his jaw muscles. I will
not allow him to ruin my cheerful mood.

The clear, sunny day brings with it feelings of lib-
eration and of sadness as I cross into Wisconsin, leaving behind my Saint Hilare Township youth.

The large sum of money Ella and I saved over
the years feels like a robber baron's bounty, bringing
with it the freedom of uninhibited adventure and the
opportunity to break free of the plains of northwestern

Minnesota, leaving behind our big farm families, made up of stern, stoic parents and many sisters and brothers. If only I could have left behind the ache from my remaining baby tooth. At eighteen years old, I should have had the adult molar replace this infantile annoyance years ago, but an inherited oddity passed down on my mother's side prevents the baby tooth from being replaced. So I am left with a toothless gap, which, thankfully, remains hidden behind my cheek, even when I smile.

"Nora." Ella's breath is in my ear, tickling, while I feel the sharp nudge of her elbow. Her eyes are filled with caution as she looks across the aisle. The businessman continues to frown in our direction, his judgmental gaze and full beard and moustache reminding me of my father.

"Don't mind him. He's just some unhappy, tired, old harrumph who ... "

"No!" Ella whispers again, more sharply, directing me to look farther up the aisle. The two young, smartly dressed gentlemen who'd bid us "Good day" as they'd boarded in Saint Paul were now tilting their heads toward each other while whispering with mischievous glances in our direction.

My face feels flush as I notice them getting up from their bench seat. "How do I look?"

"You look fine," she tells me, half convincingly. "How do I look?"

"Fine," I say, with equal assurance.

"Would you mind if we sat across from you ladies?" The taller gentleman's German accent exudes confidence.

"Not at all," I answer while Ella giggles. I give her a sharp, quick elbow.

After a short pause of settling in, he then asks, "And how far have you ladies traveled?"

"From all the way across Minnesota," I say with an air of worldliness.

"Ah, yes," he ponders. "But I can tell by your speech that your parents must be from the same old part of the world as my colleague here."

"Norway?" asks Ella.

"Sweden." I find the short, quiet gentlemen both reserved and contrite.

"Forgive me." The taller gentleman begins to tip his hat. "I am Tristan Klausmann, and this is Soren Fredrickson."

"A pleasure." The previous rush of blood to my face is now replaced with a feeling of giddiness as I attempt to change my demeanor to that more suitable for a young woman traveling across the country. "I am Nora Thorsen, and this is my dearest and oldest friend, Ella Pederson." Ella feigns a timid cough rather than a greeting, which I find slightly annoying. "And where does the train lead you gentlemen to and from?"

"We have been to the Mayo Clinic in Rochester." He adjusts his tie. "You know of it?"

"Yes. We have heard of it." I am relieved to offer pertinent information to the conversation rather than sitting like a yes-and-no ninny. "In fact, I was born in Rock Dell Township, which is very close by. So you are doctors?"

"Not quite. We are attempting to gain internship."

"Ah!" Ella smiles at Soren. "And we are off to train as nurses in New York."

"Some fine schools in New York City," he responds, still quite reserved.

"You've been there?" I ask Tristan.

"Yes. That is where we are returning to. But you ladies appear to be quite young to be adventuring into such a big city. Might I ask your ages?"

"How forward, sir," I say with a coyness attributable to women such as ourselves, far too young to be self-conscious about their age.

Just then, Ella blurts out, "I was born the day Billy the Kid was shot dead! If you know that, then you will know how old I am."

*Gracious*, I think to myself. *That was very childish, Ella.*

Tristan feigns an eerie tone. "No doubt a very ominous sign."

"Yes," says Ella, her voice bordering on shrill. "Especially when you consider he was shot in cold blood." She now looks to each of us and begins to withdraw her enthusiasm. "But no doubt educated men such as you would hardly place much stock in such things."

"On the contrary," Tristan insists. "Are you not familiar with reincarnation?"

"Oh, that's silly," I murmur, sensing his jest.

"Then you are?" he asks, his eyes now feigning seriousness.

"So you are suggesting my friend is the reincarnation of Billy the Kid?"

"According to reincarnation, is it not possible?"

We share a smile at the thought of this prospect. I feel quite relieved at how well we are conversing with such fine gentlemen.

Ella leans into the group and grabs me by the wrist. "Suddenly, I feel the urge to rob a train."

We all laugh. We share pleasantries so intimately while time passes that none of us take note of the sky's increasing darkness.

"Does it appear to anyone else that the train seems to be slowing down?" Tristan asks while looking around the car.

Soren stands up and walks toward the front of the car. When he returns, he tells us the conductor informed him the train is slowing to stay behind the storm that is quickly moving toward the east.

"Slowing a train due to a storm," Tristan says. "That is a curi-oddity, indeed."

"A 'curi' what?" asks Ella.

"Don't mind him," Soren answers, rolling his eyes. "He likes to make up his own words. Evidently, there aren't enough in the dictionary—English or German— to satisfy his dialogue."

"Seriously, am I the only one who finds this busi-ness," he responds, "both curious and odd?"

"Heavens," I say, "it's our first train ride. But I would imagine they know what they're doing."

Shortly thereafter, the train comes to a complete stop. The rain begins to fall against the roof of the now quiet passenger car.

Tristan concludes we must be on the northwesterly edge of the storm based on the movement of the mammoth storm clouds moving to the northeast. They are filled with much lightning that makes me think of the "end of days." Ella's concern is evident in her nervous fingers tapping against her knee. I carefully hide my own by covering her hand with mine while continuing to engage Tristan in small talk.

Hail begins hitting the roof and drowns out our voices, reminding me of a similar sound I would hear in the barn on the homestead while attending to chores, like the perpetual pelting of pebbles to planking, only this sound is more like large, angry rocks.

As the second wave of the storm passes, the train slowly begins its journey. As we approach our next stop, New Richmond, we can see off in the distance, to the south, destroyed farmhouses and outbuildings.

"Should the train stop to see if help is needed?" Soren wonders aloud while standing to lower the window.

"We can report what we've seen to the authorities in the town up ahead," Tristan says with an air of assurance that appears to pacify the other passengers.

As the train creeps into New Richmond, we are all shocked by the devastation that greets us. The train is forced to stop well short of the depot due to the debris strewn across both the tracks and the streets.

Word spreads quickly through the train that the small village has been struck by a powerful cyclone. Though we are advised to stay aboard the train for our own safety, the four of us agree to venture out to see what we can do to help.

Tristan is the first to step off and does so with a determination equal to that of a fireman ready to enter a blazing building in hopes of rescuing someone in distress. Soren follows with a cautious stride while Ella and I step lightly over debris, lifting the hemlines of our dresses as we go.

As our little group makes its way easterly through the light rain toward the center of the village, we can see more foundations without houses. Some have been completely lifted away, while others have windowless walls with furnishings in disarray.

"Goodness!" Ella's voice startles me as I turn and see her awestruck expression. "What is that?" She is pointing to a dark-gray figure the size of an elephant splayed out several paces away. As we walk closer, we can see that it is indeed an elephant. It lay on its side, heavy legs stilled, and wrinkled trunk outstretched, reaching for nothing.

As we round the corner of a building, a group of disheveled men, shirts drenched and dirty, anxiously exert themselves as they struggle to whittle down a large pile of debris. With ceaseless motion, they unravel the puzzle of heavy timbers and bricks and boards that once made up the building.

"Lend a hand here!" a man shouts in our direction.

Without hesitation, both Tristan and Soren jump in to help remove the obstructions covering the building's basement.

"Quiet!" We all look at Soren standing in place and follow suit. "I hear moaning!"

"It's sure to be my wife." A bedraggled-looking man, sounding both in shock and resolute, is wading through the rubble. "We're not even supposed to be here. We don't live here. We just came to see the circus."

Farther up the street, there are many bodies lying on the ground. Some are motionless, while others are rolling about in obvious pain. Thankfully, there are survivors, unhurt, attempting to aid those afflicted.

"Here's someone!" a man shouts. "Help here!"

Both Tristan and Soren begin to dig out the poor soul covered beneath the rubble. Once cleared, Tristan announces, "It's a child. Here, Nora." He cradles the child only for a moment before handing it to me. Once in my arms, I can tell that it is a boy no older than five or six. "See if you can find water over there." He points to what appears to be a park fountain. "I'll be over directly."

"Ella. Come with me." We stumble over planks and tree limbs as we make our way to the fountain. "Do you have a cloth I can use to wrap this child's head wound?"

I look to Ella for a response, but her mouth is agape while her eyes are filled with much anxiety. Her hair is damp from the light rain. A strand loosened from the grip of her bun hangs over her temple. "Ella! Do you or don't you?"

She now appears puzzled but just as quickly snaps out of her state of confusion. "I … I'm sure I do," she stammers as she rifles through her satchel. "Here!"

I do the best I can to clean the wound and then wrap the child's head with the cloth. The boy reminds me of my youngest brother, Teddy.

Tristan walks over to us just then with his sleeves rolled up and carrying his suit coat. "Have you checked for a pulse?"

"Very faint." I look directly in his face, unable to hide the concern on my own.

"You've done a nice job of bandaging that wound." He then takes the boy's wrist and feels for himself. After a moment, he sighs. "Afraid he's gone now."

I look to Ella, who gasps and quickly spins away.

"No sign of the child's parents?" Tristan asks.

"No doubt over there." I point to the pile the men are continuing to undo.

We begin to walk back down the main street. Tristan carries the child.

We come upon a woman who is assisting with the wounded. She tells us her husband, a doctor, is attending to the injured at one of the nearby churches left standing. She urgently asks us to follow her with the child.

"My cat was acting amiss all afternoon," she tells us, slowly shaking her head. "I guess they sense things the rest of us don't."

Ella and I help in the makeshift hospital while Tristan and Soren continue to help dig out survivors and administer aid. Supplies are short, as two of the four local doctors' buildings have been destroyed.

The track is cleared just before midnight, when we are asked to reboard so that our train can continue on its journey and allow the relief train to take its place at the destroyed depot.

While the others sleep to the sound of the train's rhythmic pulse, I pull out my sketchpad and begin drawing some of the things I had seen. The night sky is now clear, and the moonlight gives me a feeling of the macabre as I repeatedly shift from my memories of the day and back to the pad. I had read years earlier the account of a Civil War soldier who had done this very same thing after witnessing the horrors of battle in hopes of putting his mind at ease through documentation and illustration.

Ella's head rests on my shoulder as I make short strokes outlining the merchant's building devastated on the main street of New Richmond. The weight of her head feels light and becomes lighter with each of her long inhalations. I am glad to see her so relaxed. Neither Ella's parents nor mine spoke of how I should make every effort to protect Ella, but, instead, this obligation is something I place on myself. And after today's ominous events, the responsibility feels more acute than I imagined. The presence of Tristan and Soren seated across from us cheers me greatly. It is both a sad and a good day. This is how life will be from now on, and I embrace this notion, for I know that it is God's will.

We are all very tired when we arrive in New York City's Grand Central Station very late the day after the cyclone. In spite of the late hour, there are many people running to and fro. And though we are quite fatigued from the previous day's traumatic experience, Ella and I are excited by all the sights and sounds of the city.

"Ladies," Soren begins, "the unpleasantness of this journey was most assuredly offset by your presence."

"I give second motion to that," says Tristan with the most enchanting of smiles. "The two of you have the makings of fine nurses."

Our new friends are quite helpful in providing us with both direction and transport to our boardinghouse. We exchange good-byes and make assurances that we will meet up again soon.

We are greeted at the door by the landlady, a Mrs. Gorman, who is quite unhappy to be aroused so late at night.

"This is highly irregular," she says, pulling the collar of her housecoat tightly around her neck. "Curfew is eight o'clock for young ladies."

"We were delayed by the calamities out West," I explain, taking great pains not to offend. "Surely you heard about it."

"Calamities, you say?" She appears perplexed. Just then a cat dashes between Ella and me in an obvious attempt to gain access through the front door. "I see you're out late too, Oscar!" she shouts back over her shoulder. Then she turns back to us. "Always, you westerners with your calamities. Gun play, no doubt, and little doggies to lasso. Can't you people join the rest of us as we enter the new century?"

We are far too tired to argue and, instead, beg her for directions to our room.

"Number eight. Third floor. Key's in the lock."

Our room is no less and no more than we expected. There are two single beds, each with its own nightstand, a desk and chair, and a dresser and mirror that will have to accommodate both Ella's and my belongings. I see my bedraggled reflection in the mirror change from shaded to glowing as the electric lamp slowly illuminates the room. I don't recognize myself so far from home.

The wallpaper is a dingy white with a small, pale blue flower pattern. The light brown hardwood floors are rough where footwear has traveled most and much more dark and shiny near the walls and beneath the dresser.

The one window gives us a view of a solid-brick wall of the building across the alley. The sun will visit our room only a few hours a day, I suspect.

"Nora," Ella whispers, her voice sounding somber. She is slumped in the only chair in the room.

"Yes?"

"I'm not sure I'm ready for this."

"What do you mean?"

"This," she answers, looking up while raising her palms to the ceiling. "All of this."

"What's the matter, Ella?"

"I didn't want to appear so childish today in front of our new friends, but now that we're alone…"

Her head droops, and her body collapses like a worn-out rag doll. I walk over to her, kneel on the floor, and take her hands into mine. "You did wonderfully. We helped so many people yesterday. That should make you happy."

"It does." Tears begin to stream down her cheeks. "But I'm not as strong as you. You seem to have a better hold on your faith when it comes to…" She pauses while still breathing heavily. "Death," I say, helping her avoid saying the word.

"Yes. I may not be strong enough for this." She pulls from beneath the front of her dress the nurse's emblem attached to a chain given to her by her grandmother.

I wrap my arms around her shoulders and kiss her on the cheek. I hear various noises outside our window coming from the street below. We will have to acclimate ourselves to our new surroundings.

"He was so young, so frail." She lifts the nurse's emblem to her lips.

"We'll sleep tonight. Let's not think about such things." I lift her head by the chin, smile, and speak softly, looking into her eyes, "Weeping may remain for a night, but rejoicing comes in the morning."

The following morning does indeed bring much rest and relief. Even our landlady is obviously filled with something most spiritual, as we awake to her singing melodically but also quite loudly.

"Did I hear the word *Weihnachtsbaume*?" Ella asks. I notice her complexion to be very radiant this morning.

"Yes." I smile. "She is singing about Christmas and winter in the middle of June."

We laugh but quickly shush each other. We have no desire to make our year-long stay unpleasant by gaining the wrong side of our landlady.

Our first full day in New York is on the Sabbath. After enjoying a most hardy breakfast presented by the now more even-tempered Mrs. Gorman, Ella and I venture out into our neighborhood in search of the nearest Lutheran church.

"The first thing," my mother instructed me, "is to find a proper place of sanctuary in line with your faith. Once you have done that, my daughter, you will find all other things fall into place just as God intended."

Ella and I arrive late to the ten o'clock service and sit near the back. We pray for those victims in the little village of New Richmond.

# These Little Ones

See that you do not look down on one of these little ones. For I tell you that their angels in heaven always see the face of my Father in heaven.

Matthew 18:10

Our first week in New York City finds both Ella and I laboring under the crushing weight of varied cultures and customs. People who have adapted to the city long before our arrival are quick to seek our attention to peddle their wares. I imagine we must look like easy prey, out-of-towners without an ounce of sensibility. At first, we are cautious, careful not to stray far from our own neighborhood, but find it too tempting not to venture into some of the nearby surroundings.

A trolley ride brings us to the market on Mulberry Street. The smell of this part of the city is that of coal and with a hint of outhouse, I'm afraid. There are many vendor stands lining both sides of the street, managed by mostly men, selling various goods, clothing, and kitchenware. Ella wishes to try on an elegant hat that I suggest is beyond both our class and price. I find myself longing for a pair of shoes of the latest fashion.

"Look at what we have at our disposal, Ella. All our wants and needs can be fulfilled right here."

"Except an abundance of money," she reminds me with a look of caution that subdues my ecstatic tone.

An Italian man wearing a black bowler cap and blue suspenders wishes to sell us a meat grinder made of sturdy wood and with a handle the color of gold. Besides his asking all of two dollars for the grinder, we are unable to discern what he is saying, but I believe him to be both an honest and flirtatious fellow. We decline with cheerful smiles as we move on.

Not all of our encounters are so pleasant. While strolling down past the market, we cross the path of a group of ill-kempt men playing a sort of coin game in the middle of the sidewalk. When we request the right of way, they give us the most unfriendly stares while we stroll by. Once past, we are greeted with similar scowls from a group of women seated on the steps of the nearby tenement. The only happy faces this side of the market are those of the children playing in the streets.

I am thankful for the sturdy breeze finding its way down the back alley and into our little boarding room. I lay on Ella's bed, resting my eyes as the sun slowly sets behind the neighboring building.

"Goodness, Nora, what have we gotten ourselves into?"

"It's not a country school, Ella. I'll give you that."

"But this Latin, of what use is it?"

"It is part of the curriculum. Besides, I'd hoped to learn many languages over time."

"Oh, but that is just you, Nora. As long as I can remember, you've been picking up phrases from this and that language. French. Spanish. And even a little Russian."

"*Ja Bortsett fra nei fin omgangsspråk enn Norsk.*"

"Yes, Nora. But no finer language than Norwegian."

We laugh, but then Ella quietly lies down, and our voices drift away, out the window. I find myself reflecting upon the past day and the characters that are to instruct us on how to become proper nurses.

Professor Greenwald, our Latin instructor, possesses a dour disposition, which is displayed with drooping eyes and a rolling chin sidled by a salt-and-pepper mutton-chop beard. I sensed his disdain for students the very first day. Or perhaps he is merely envious of our youth. From my textbook, I piece together a phrase to match his sad face: *Ut iuvenescit.* To be young again.

Professor Moore is a thinly built man who only half fills out his attire and possesses greasy, dark hair and a notable vein running vertically near the center of his forehead. These disturbing features are apropos, I conclude, as he is responsible for teaching anatomy and does so alongside the skeleton of an unnamed woman who, we are told, was found floating in the Hudson River some years ago.

Professor Van der Dyke, our biology instructor, approaches the class in a sardonic yet whimsical manner. There is a sense of indifference to life and the living as his displaced spectacles tip precariously on the tip of his nose. His gray hair is disheveled, and his stained, off-white lab coat smells rather musty, I imagine, even from my vantage point halfway across the room.

I am about to remind Ella of the smelly lab coat when she interrupts. "I'm not so sure I can manage watching an autopsy, Nora."

"That's a long ways off, so don't worry about it now, my dear."

"I still think about the other day. There were so many people killed."

"Yes. I know. It was the will of God."

"I suppose you're right. But the thought of so many people dying… It's so much easier to consider when it's news from far off but something entirely different when you're caught up in it."

I am begging Ella to no longer dwell on the experience just as the downstairs bell rings, summoning us to supper.

"I've an appetite!" Ella pushes her chair out from under the desk. "Hurry along, Nora. Remember what Mrs. Gorman says about being on time for meals."

As I sit up, I scrunch my face and alter my voice. "'All young ladies make haste, or their food will go to waste.' How was that?"

"Frightening." Ella feigns an expression of fear. "Particularly your facial contortion. You better not let Mrs. Gorman hear you mocking her."

⚜

After two weeks in New York, and after managing our studies properly, we are finally able to engage our friends from the train, Tristan and Soren. However, I grow apprehensive at our decision to become better acquainted with these gentlemen. Although I find them both charming and attractive, I am very concerned by Tristan's undermining of my faith through what he refers to as the philosophical sciences.

"If you understand Schopenhauer," he rallies as we enjoy tea at a very quaint coffeehouse, "you understand that life is about suffering. And to counter this suffering, man looks to the aesthetic, that which provides a view of life that tends to disguise all the suffering."

"And what part does faith in God play in this scenario you describe?" My tone is quite curt at this point. And my bad tooth begins to throb, which does nothing to improve my mood.

"Faith in God is but another form of aesthetics. If you are considering the spiritual world, then you are not really partaking of the sufferings of the physical world. Surely, Nora, you can see that." I detect more than a hint of condescension in his somewhat apologetic chuckle.

"But if my faith is founded in compassion for my fellow human being," I counter, roused and emphatic, "then how can I not be focused on the physical world?"

"Agreed." Tristan's eyes are seemingly filled with caution at first but then quickly replaced with confidence. "Compassion plays a very strong role in the world we exist in. I believe the four of us demonstrate this through our studies and endeavors to become doctors and nurses. But now think about your motivation to be a nurse. Is it founded solely in altruism, a desire to help others? I think you would agree that there is more to it than that."

"Yes, there is something more to it, but I am not so sure I would agree that it is this 'will to live' business you refer to." Tristan is a dullard, I conclude, if he cannot read the irritation etched on my face.

"Then," he says as he waves off the subject, finally sensing my aggravation, "I shouldn't trouble you with the notion of the 'absurdity of life.'"

"My head is spinning." Ella waves her hands about her head as though she is shooing away a disagreeable fly. "Would you be so kind, Soren, to pour me another cup of tea?"

"My pleasure." Soren nearly spills his own tea cup while quickly reaching for the pot.

"If I might speak," Ella says, "I think it remains important for people everywhere to feel beholden to their fellow man. A simple notion from a simple country girl."

Instantly, Soren's eyes light up as his knee accidentally bumps against the bottom of our table. "Now you are speaking to my philosophical leanings." He lifts his cup in toast. "To Kierkegaard. And not just because we share the same first name. But because we both share the belief that life is about how one lives rather than how one thinks."

"That's nice," Ella says. "To Kierkegaard."

"To Kierkegaard," I emphasize by extending my cup in Tristan's face. "Whoever he is, I like how he thinks."

Appearing dejected, Tristan's shoulders slump toward the table while his chin drops down into his free palm, and resignedly, he toasts with us. "To God's little Danish brother."

It is a relief to find that he does not take himself so seriously all the time. In fact, there are times I wish I could feel toward Tristan as Ella does toward Soren. Alas, may she take as much care as I shall.

❦

*July 1899*

As Ella and I walk the streets with our gentlemen friends, we come across a multitude of protesters; the most astonishing part is they are made up mostly of children. As we gather nearer the periphery, I can hear the voice of one of the boys as he stands above all the others. As I peer through the gathering crowd, I can see a boy wearing an eye patch beginning to speak.

"Frien's and feller workers," he begins, "Dis is a time which tries de hearts of men. Dis is de time when we'se got to stick together like glue. We know wot we wants, and we'll git it, even if we is blind."

I tap the shoulder of one of the lads in front of me and inquire as to the problem.

"They's stealing from us blind, miss. Ten cents more they's wants. For every bundle."

"Who is?" asks Ella.

"De big pockets. De ones who run the places. Here and over on Forty-second."

"Newspapers," Tristan mutters in my ear, sounding indifferent.

"Don't you think there is something to it? Could all these children be standing here for want of nothing better to do?"

"This is the way of the city, Nora. As they say, you can't fight city hall."

"If it's city hall's responsibility, then they should be brought to bear for what is happening. Don't you see the same things as I?"

"These are the poorest of the poor. It's merely their lot in life."

"Should anyone's lot be that of wandering through the city without a decent pair of shoes or clothing?"

"What is all this about?" a finely dressed, elderly gentlemen carrying a cane inquires. His accent is decidedly French.

"Some trouble with the hired help," Tristan relays, taking me by the arm to continue walking. "Storm in a teacup."

"I should say not." I pull my elbow from his grasp as I feel a surge of anger running up the back of my spine. "These poor children are protesting for their very right to survive. And I suspect the ink on *their* hands is just as real as the dirt found under the fingernails of any other day-laborer."

"I see." The Frenchman appears quizzical as he strokes his graying beard with fingertips stained the color of brown.

"I assure you, sir," Tristan continues, "this is the sort of thing the authorities do not need to be bothered with."

"I disagree emphatically."

Before I can explain further, I am interrupted by the Frenchman. "Your most charming lady friend appears to disagree with your assessment of the situation."

I am quite flattered by the Frenchman's compliment. Just as I am about to solicit his name, a great commotion begins only paces from us.

"The goons!" shouts Soren. "They're beating back the children!"

Before I can give Tristan a piece of my mind, one of the "goons" makes his way between us, pushing Tristan in one direction and me in the other. Fortuitously, our French acquaintance avails himself to catch me in his arms as I fall backward. I look over my shoulder and stare up into his brown eyes. He gives me a brief smile and then sets me to his side.

"Move on, you lot!" The goon strikes a formidable pose with bare forearms that give note of how serious he is about his position. "Keep this area clear."

"On whose orders?" snaps Tristan as he straightens his jacket.

"On the orders of the owner himself, Mr. Hearst, that's who." Then he turns in Soren's direction. "And what are you going to do about it?"

The Frenchman taps the brute's shoulder from behind with his cane. "Your pardon, dear sir."

The bully turns and growls, "You'll want no part of me, Frenchy."

"And you'll not want any part of my cutlass," he murmurs and begins to twist the brass handle of his staff.

The bully puzzles over the Frenchman, looks around for his companions, and, spotting them, makes a sudden retreat in their direction.

"That was a sticky predicament, we should all agree," the Frenchman says with both an air of triumph and relief.

"Goodness, sir," I say, equally relieved yet quite impressed with the man's steadfastness.

"Indeed," begins Tristan. "Would you have really run that man through?"

"Hardly." He chuckles. "Even had I *had* a cutlass hidden in this old cane of mine."

"Would have served the devil right," Soren interjects while stroking his lapels.

"Where are all the boys going?" Ella wonders aloud.

"They seem to be breaking up for the moment," Tristan notes, "as instructed."

Then I hear chanting coming from the front of the crowd as it moves down the street in the direction of Union Square.

"I suspect they'll be back this way again tomorrow," the Frenchman predicts.

"How can you be so sure after how they were just treated?" I ask.

"Any cause, dear lady, worth fighting for, et cetera, et cetera." He waves his hand in the air for hollow emphasis. "Viva liberty!"

The Frenchman strolls alongside us, and just as Tristan is about to tip his hat to bid *adieu*, he speaks. "Well, that was exciting. But now I find myself quite thirsty." He looks into my eyes. "I would very much like to offer to buy you and your friends a drink."

"But, *monsieur*," I protest. "It's we who should buy you a drink for your quick and decisive action."

"But that is nonsense, *ma cherie*. I am a man of the world who is growing older by the minute and would most enjoy, at my expense, making the acquaintance of such fine young people. Allow me to introduce myself," he says while tipping his hat. "My name is Auguste Valadon."

After we introduce ourselves, Tristan, looking rather quizzical, now asks, "You are, indeed, the *artist* Valadon?"

"It is true," he responds as we step into a modest restaurant near the corner of Broadway. "That you recognize me *sans palette*, I am honored."

"This is an honor, Monsieur Valadon," I say. "Unlike our escorts, my companion and I are simple farm girls from the Midwest United States."

"The honor is all mine, ladies," he says with a smile. "And may I add that you two are the most enjoyable surprise I have had during my stay in New York?"

"And how long have you been in the city?" asks Ella.

"Since early spring. I have committed myself to a year in New York in an attempt to challenge my craft, capture the nuances and subtleties that make up this ever-expanding metropolis. However, as things are, I wish to return to Paris sooner. New York, I have learned, is not a city of lovers of art or, for that matter, lovers, present company excluded, I'm sure. It's more a city of petty bureaucrats, faux aristocrats, and sleepless tomcats."

I laugh with Monsieur Valadon.

"But you two charming young ladies," he continues, "I must first capture on canvas. With the permission of your suitors, that is."

"I assure you, dear sir, we are not spoken for." I make this point with great emphasis by throwing my shoulders back while lifting my chin high. "We are what are known as liberated women."

"Please, Nora, don't begin again with your suffrage ramblings," says Tristan with a strained grin. He seems to have turned surly since our encounter with Monsieur Valadon.

"Don't mind the ladies, sir," says Soren, smiling. "Whatever they say is merely the parroting of things heard from a street corner this morning."

"*Au contraire*, my good man," explains Monsieur Valadon. "The tides of equality are crossing the continent of Europe. Mark my words; soon it will be as such here in your colonies."

"Nora sketches!" Ella blurts out.

"Ella!" I grab her wrist, wanting more to throttle her neck, but I am glad she disrupts the conversation's flow toward the political.

"Does she now? I should like to see some of your work."

"I assure you, sir, they are mere chicken scratching. Something you could just as easily find in the street outside the front door."

"But you'll allow me to judge for myself, won't you?"

I quickly speak for both Ella and myself as I express how exciting it would be to have our portrait painted by such a well-known artist direct from the environs of Paris and by the end of our encounter agree to spend the next several weekend mornings in monsieur Valadon's rented studio.

❧

The wide street and the two-story brick buildings lining either side along Varick Street in Greenwich Village gives this part of New York a sense of openness. How nice it is to be in an area where there are not so many people and where the buildings are not so tall as to blot the sunlight most of the day.

A horse-drawn wagon travels from building to building making early morning deliveries.

Monsieur Valadon opens the door to greet us as we make our way up the stoop.

"Good morning, ladies." His mood is cheerful as I continue to take in his neighborhood.

"Good morning, Monsieur Valadon," I respond. "What a wonderful setting you have here right in the city. It's tranquil yet still urban."

"Yes," adds Ella. "It is quite charming, monsieur."

"Best of all," he continues while holding the door, "the morning light is perfect for indoor portraits. However, before we continue, one thing we must agree on is that you ladies must call me by my given name, Auguste."

I smile at our host just as Ella observes, "I believe your milk deliveryman is here, monsieur."

"Oh, he is here for the downstairs woman. Come in, ladies. Come in."

The lighting is, indeed, quite bright as I enter the large one-room studio where windows extend the length of the room while reaching high to the ceiling. There are several canvases lining the far wall and several others on the floor. A long and messy table to the left of the room holds many glass containers filled with liquids and powders. And to the right, a curtain covers what I believe to be Auguste's bed and personal effects.

"Might we see your paintings before we start, monsieur?" asks Ella.

"Auguste, my dear girl."

"Auguste," she corrects herself.

"Where is this from?" I ask, gazing upon a very dark landscape of a harbor, which strikes me as desolate.

"Down on the Battery, overlooking the East River. You can see Governor's Island off in the distance."

"We've never been there," I explain.

"Such a big city," Ella adds. "So much to see."

"Nothing to see down on the Battery. I think I painted this more as a reminder than an attempt to capture something beautiful."

"How so a reminder?" I ask.

"It's a reminder of how young yet dark the nature of this city is. See the ships and boats lining the piers?"

Ella and I both nod.

"There is little color to capture in this scene. It's almost as if the city is still in search of its own internal beauty."

"I can see," Ella notes, "that even the sunlight does not help bring brightness to dark grays and browns that make up the structures in this picture, but that seems natural."

"Natural in New York, my dear Ella, but not so much in Paris. I wish I could explain it better. Perhaps a sense of longitude would help, but we shouldn't let this lighting get away from us, so I will forego the geography lesson for the moment."

But Ella continues the discussion by asking, "Couldn't you find more suitable scenes in Central Park that would provide a … a … "

"Spark?"

"Yes. Exactly."

"These might be what you're thinking of." He thumbs through a number of medium-sized canvases leaning against the wall. They have color and definition both Ella and I find refreshing, but Auguste makes note of his disapproval and waves them off without explanation. "I did these when I first arrived in the city. They were done with zeal, but now I am no longer moved by them."

"Could it be, Auguste," I ask, "that you're homesick?"

"Very perceptive, my dear."

*August 1899*

The evening air is mild and calm, replaced by a stillness of the usual hustle of the neighborhood. The locals are engaged in passive conversations, the memory of the workday replaced by attentive listening and sincere laughter. Only the starlings remain active, swooping and gliding between buildings, finally resting on the many clotheslines stretched above the street. I find myself drifting back to the homestead while sitting on the steps outside the boardinghouse. I pretend the steps are those of the front porch of the farmhouse. I picture the hay fields to the east, rolling from the northwesterly breeze, which signals an oncoming storm, while pretending to hear the sound of rustling leaves in the big elm trees that line the dirt road to the north.

I ask myself, *How can I make the two places—city and country—come together as one? How can I seam chaos and tranquility?* The moment of commingling the two is both fleeting and unattainable. I break from the trance upon hearing the paused steps of a passerby. I look up to see Tristan standing at the foot of the stoop.

"Good evening, Nora." His coat jacket is flung over his shoulder, and his dress-shirt sleeves are rolled up to his elbows. I notice his broad smile and feel my eyes smiling in return.

"Where did you come from?"

"I was in the mood for a walk and found myself passing down your street. And what luck that I should find you here, although as I came closer, you looked as though your thoughts were far away."

"I was just thinking of home."

"Good thoughts, I trust?"

"Always."

He rests his hand on the stoop's emerald-colored adornment while scraping the sole of his shoe against the first step. "Could I persuade you to join me in a walk?"

"Certainly."

"This is a familiar setting, you will agree, Nora." Tristan, seemingly reading my thoughts, notes my reflective state as we stroll through Central Park. "Perhaps a reminder of your homeland?"

"Yes. In many ways, I should agree with you, although there are far fewer vendors scattered about my father's acreage."

"And do the fields produce corn as tasty as this?" We smile at one another as he hands me a bag of popcorn.

"Our fields are mostly wheat and barley."

After quickly scanning our surroundings, he shrugs. "And not one bread or beer vendor in sight for comparison's sake, I'm afraid."

A smartly dressed couple astride a two-seat bicycle clumsily glides past us while negotiating the hill up ahead with disorderly shouts filled with laughter.

"How are your studies, Nora? You are available this school night, so I imagine things are quite well?"

"They are challenging yet manageable." I can't help but smile at the bicyclists.

"And Ella? She is well?"

"Quite well. In fact, I believe she is seeing Soren this evening."

"You are correct. He is quite taken with her."

"And she should experience new things." I point up ahead. "Look! They almost toppled over."

"I'd hardly consider my good friend Soren a thing."

"I'm sorry, Tristan. I didn't mean to offend."

"Well… And how is your painting exercise with Monsieur Valadon?" I detect a note of jealousy in his tone.

"It is a tedious business, but the excitement of the end production keeps us involved. I wish I could describe Monsieur Valadon's progress, but he does not allow us to see. He believes we will be all the more astonished at the final result."

Our steps are gently paced as we continue down several streets leading toward lower Manhattan. Tristan tells of his adventures in the city and how it is such a beautiful place to fall in love. Whether he is eluding to something between himself and me or our friends' involvement, I can't say. So I make a point of emphasizing how any romance Ella may be experiencing can only be short lived, as she and I have big plans for the future.

"But, Nora, life has a way of altering the future. I mean, dreams appear vivid and real enough when one devotes all attention to them, but reality has a strange way of interceding."

"I am tempted to give you some leeway on this point but would prefer not to debate it on such a lovely evening."

"Agreed. That you and I are sharing a relaxing stroll is but a dream come true in and of itself." At this, Tristan graciously offers me his arm. I gladly accept but with some reservation, as I do not wish to give him the wrong impression.

"I do believe these buildings are some of the more grand that I have come across."

"Oh, yes. This is part of the city that continues to expand with the vibrations of commerce and industry. This building here looks to be in the process of topping them all with its height and depth."

I am always impressed with all the large buildings, these works of art made up of so much brick and curved bay windows, giving the illusion of both strength and fragility. They are a far cry from the tenements of the Lower East End, where so many immigrants are crammed into small tinderboxes.

As we walk along the periphery of the construction site, I notice a middle-aged man looking forlorn, seated on a plank bench near a pile of rubble. Our shadows fall upon him, breaking his reverie. He looks up at us, his eyes now glinting as we pass by. "*Han er tapt.*"

"Who?" I ask. "*Hvem er tapt?* Who is lost?"

"*Min bror.*"

"What is he saying, Nora?"

"He says his brother is lost."

"Do you need help, sir?" asks Tristan.

"It is too late." The man points to the rubble nearby.

"Do you mean to say your brother is trapped beneath all these rocks?"

"Yes. The hoist broke, and the heavy granite fell on him."

"Why are there no men digging him out?" I ask.

"It is impossible tonight. A new hoist is needed to lift the heavy pieces, but it will not be here 'til tomorrow."

"But why are you here?" I ask.

"He is my brother. I need to stay by his side 'til I can take him back to Minnesota."

"Minnesota." I sit down next to the man. "I am from Minnesota, sir."

"I thought you might be. It is nice to see a friendly face from back home."

Tristan begins to root around in the rubble, able to move only the smaller pieces of granite.

"I am very sorry about your brother." I place my hand upon the man's arm.

"Thank you, miss. He was the only brother I had." His voice quivers in a near whisper. "We traveled everywhere together. We worked on many farms and then on the railroad."

"And your travels brought you all the way to New York?"

"Yes. We worked for the railroad in Minnesota for many months. It was good work, but when we heard the train was hauling granite all the way to New York, my brother wished to go see the big city."

I half smile at the man, wishing to convey sorrow. "My name is Nora."

"I am Knute." He pats my hand while shuffling the soles of his worn, dusty boots against gravel where men sweat for a day's pay.

"I think your brother's wish to venture so far from Minnesota speaks highly of his character." I hear the brittle tone of doubt in my own voice, wishing now to retract my unqualified praise.

"How do you mean?" Knute's expression is half insult, half bewilderment.

"He's … a … dreamer," I stammer, sounding even more insincere, I'm afraid. "What I mean is, he was not afraid to be adventurous, to experience what life had to offer."

"I never thought about that. I have only been thinking of how strange it is that my brother would be crushed by the thing that tempted him to venture so far from home in the first place."

I find Knute's revelation disheartening. My stomach begins to churn with anxiety and uncertainty. Did Tristan and I come upon Knute and the tragic end of his brother by chance? I feel something akin to a premonition seething just beneath my sense of reality, but one I cannot wrap my mind around.

Now Tristan stands before us, brushing granite dust from his hands while his eyes suggest he has arrived to save me from my inarticulateness. "Shall we continue on, Nora?"

As I begin to rise, I place my hand on Knute's shoulder. "I shall pray for you and your brother, dear friend."

"Thank you, miss." Knute bows his head as I rise.

I have little to say as Tristan and I walk back to the boardinghouse.

"I'm so sorry, Nora, that the evening was spoiled by such bad news. I had no idea we would come across such a tragedy."

"Nonsense, Tristan. How were you to know?"

"But you're obviously distraught by what you've seen this evening."

"That is true. I can't help but think how devastated I would be if anything ever happened to Ella. She is, after all, like a sister to me, so I can completely understand Knute's devotion and loyalty to his dearly departed brother."

"But what could possibly happen? You're both very sensible young women, not inclined to make foolish decisions or choices, which is evidenced by your desire to share the company of Soren and myself."

I smile at Tristan's feeble attempt at humor as we continue our walk toward Broadway, where the motion of crowds and horse carriages provide both a welcome distraction and a reminder of future expectations.

*September 1899*

During the presentation of the portrait, Auguste takes great care to place the painting in the most favorable light. It is quite becoming. The first thing I notice is Ella and I sharing the same hairstyle and color, a strawberry blonde, which Auguste has taken the liberty of letting down. Auguste has made mine appear a touch more auburn by casting the lightest shading across the top half of my head, over both my eyes and the bridge of my nose, and atop my opposite shoulder. It makes me appear as the older of the two. My disposition is noticeably serious with just the hint of worldliness, which I appreciate most sincerely.

Ella, positioned just behind my right shoulder, by contrast, appears almost angelic, with her head slightly tilted toward my inside shoulder. She stands beneath the shading, her dark-blue eyes gazing past the front of me.

"What am I looking at so far off?" asks Ella, her voice decidedly filled with as much pride as the glowing moon. "Whatever it is, it seems to be making me sad."

"Yes," Auguste. "The eyes reveal much in a painting. I'm not sure what you are contemplating. It's just the look seemed apropos for your personality."

"And mine?" I ask, reserving judgment.

"Nora, you know perfectly well yours is that of confidence and determination."

⁂

The clanging bell from a fire brigade crashing by wakes me. I see the flickering shadows from the street lamp outside dancing through the drapes upon the wall. I am now restless. I think about what Ella was eluding to just before we turned out the light. She tempered her excitement, no doubt, because she could sense my simmering impatience.

*"But it's something that needs to be said."*

*"Nothing needs to be said. Everything is as it should be."*

*"You're being silly, Nora. Things, important things, should always be spoken between good friends. I would want to hear about you and Tristan…"*

*"Don't even think it," I interrupt, concluding the conversation. "Anyway, I'm very tired and wish to go to sleep."*

I am filling my head with knowledge to the point of bursting, and all for the sake of independence. I am committed to the path chosen, I'm certain, by God Himself, a path laid down over the years by a vision as hard and true as a railroad track. I'll allow nothing to derail it.

I now roll over to my side, agitated, swishing my hair over my ear while looking across the room through the darkness, staring at Ella as she lies, angelic and peaceful. I begin to wonder how she came to this point so quickly. Of course, I know the culprit by name— Soren. Something like a match ignites in the back of my mind. I whisper, "Don't you even dare!"

⚜

Last night has been forgotten, erased as though our conversation had never occurred. We have spent a beautiful Saturday morning strolling streets that grow more familiar with each passing day.

Now Ella leads me down a new, unfamiliar street.

"I've never been here before," she says with a broad smile, "but I am told we will find its atmosphere most entertaining."

The noise is near deafening.

"And what does this remind you of?" She knows me well enough to read both my mind and my smile, I think.

I notice the tip of her tongue shifting to the side of her slightly parted lips while her eyes slowly move back and forth. "I'm not sure what you mean," she says with a brow askew.

The cacophony of pianos playing different notes all at once is both chaotic energy and horrifying to the ears.

"Well?" I ready myself for an insult.

Now her expression turns to that of enlightenment. "I think it reminds me of your efforts, only a thousand times worse."

"I knew you'd say that." I find her jest refreshing rather than spiteful. "I don't have an ear for music, so I am able to appreciate this racket because it is so much like my own."

"Soren is right. This street's nickname is appropriate."

I shudder at the sound of his name. Ignoring it, I say, "Tin Pan Alley could easily be the name used to describe my mother's kitchen while a Sunday feast is prepared for the multitudes."

"How anyone can practice with so much noise around them..."

"A wonder, indeed." We stroll along for several blocks, arm-in-arm, finally rounding a familiar corner, where the smells of freshly baked goods arouse my appetite. The two of us come to this little bakery shop often to partake of the pastries that remind us of home.

The proprietor greets us with his usual enthusiasm. "The painting is finished, no?" He sets two glasses of water on our table and then begins to fumble with his icing-stained apron.

"Yes, Henri," I say, feeling a bit prideful. "Our images have been immortalized."

"Or," Ella cautiously interjects, "at least bestowed the privilege of hanging in some obscure setting, though I can't imagine where."

"My establishment, if you prefer!" Henri's expression is both enthusiastic and earnest as his puffy, bearded face ponders the walls of his shop. "Such an honor it would be to have the painting of such beautiful ladies by such a great artist from my homeland for all to see."

"You're too kind, Henri." My cheeks begin to tingle.

After placing our order for freshly made apple pie, I consider asking Auguste if he would allow the painting to be hung in Ella's and my room, at least until he is ready to return to France.

"I'm going to miss our little walks, Nora." I note a peculiar look on Ella's face, one reminding me of a Cheshire cat.

"What are you saying?" My curiosity is piqued. "Our walks? What do you mean?"

"I have news to tell you!"

"Yes. I can see that you do." I begin to grow irritated.

"There is the sound of wedding bells in the air!"

"Wedding. Whose wedding?"

"Don't you understand, Nora? I've decided to return home."

A wave of disbelief washes over me. My eyes dart from table to table, judging the couples seated around me. I suddenly feel contempt for their presence.

"Soren has proposed to me, and I've decided to move back home and wait for him while he completes his internship at the Mayo Clinic."

My words spring forth like a mid-day shower upon unsuspecting picnickers. "But what do you know of married life, Ella? And how do you know you will even make a good wife or Soren a good husband?"

"We are in love. Isn't that enough to build a marriage upon?"

I feel betrayed. My future passes before my eyes, jolted and jumbled, just as Henri sets our plates down. I stare at the slice of pie, its shape and form all too familiar now, reminding me of the past that belongs in the past. "Yours are empty promises," I say. "You've no consideration for my thoughts and feelings." Just as the words slip out, I begin to feel very ashamed.

"Please don't act this way," she pleads.

This may be good news on several counts, but I am being difficult for my own selfish reasons. Ella and I had been nearly attached at the hip our whole lives. I never imagined either of one us marrying, particularly so young.

"I am very sorry, Ella." I muster a smile. "I must sound so stupid. Congratulations to you and Soren both."

"Thank you, Nora." She smiles, but her eyes are filled with hurt.

"When are you going home, Ella?"

"I have a train ticket to leave next Sunday."

*So soon*, I think. "You should have told me long before now, Ella." Again, I sound short and hurt, but I catch myself. "We'll spend the coming Saturday together as well," I finally say, "and see the sights before you leave."

❧

I am able to make eye contact with Tristan while he is gathered outside a lecture hall with a group of his peers. I wave to him with both vigor and urgency. I fumble with my handbag while he dashes toward me with a look of concern.

"Is everything all right, Nora?" I flinch when he places his hand on my shoulder. I quickly compose myself and force a smile. "You look quite upset."

"Oh, nonsense. I was just passing by and noticed you standing, engaged in conversation. I didn't mean to interrupt." I am apprehensive as to how to the broach the subject of Ella and Soren's engagement. "How was the lecture?"

"Very interesting and insightful. The topic was mental illness." With a reflective gaze, he strokes his chiseled jaw with fingers honed to precision. "A little too illustrative concerning the treatment, however. Particularly the discussion of leucotomy, of which I shall spare you the details." He smiles.

"I'm glad." I struggle to make eye contact. My thoughts are transfixed on one topic.

"Please tell me what has you so vexed, Nora."

"Soren and Ella."

"Their engagement?" His eyes smile with approval.

"So you knew?" Astonished, I imagine everyone has been told except me.

"Yes. Soren spoke of it this morning. I think it's wonderful news, don't you?"

"Very unexpected, I should think."

"Perhaps to the unobservant."

I take offense at this remark, clenching my jaw as I look away from him.

"What I meant, Nora, is..."

"I know what you meant. Someone, even with eyes shut, should have foreseen the inevitable. I, on the other hand, have deliberately chosen to turn a blind eye."

"I can't understand why, Nora."

"I'm not sure I could explain it to you, Tristan, even if I knew myself," I lie. The moment grows awkward as I realize how alone I am in my point of view.

"Would you like to go somewhere to sit and discuss your concerns?"

I realize the pointlessness in soliciting Tristan's advice or intervention in the matter. He is, after all, of the same ilk. I lie yet again, this time about a prior commitment, and bid him a good evening.

⚜

Ella and I take advantage of a beautiful Saturday, a stolen day absent of studies and new acquaintances, and spend the early afternoon picnicking in Liberty Park, and then we take the ferry to Liberty Island to see the statue up close.

Once we have paid for our tickets, we make our way up the spiral staircase along with several other visitors.

I have never been so high in all my life. I can see Brooklyn Bridge straight out from the windows of the crown but cannot sight Ellis Island. I imagine how my parents had come through New York on their way out west before this great lady was erected. I intend to provide a first-hand description in my next letter home.

As we view the distant horizon, I tell Ella how I wish we could ascend to the flame so we could feel a part of it, burning brightly, incessantly, eternally.

"How prideful," she says. "Don't include me. I'm just here to see the city from this spectacular height."

"Oh, Ella," I whisper, "don't be such a bore."

"What do you mean?" she whispers in return.

"I don't think you understand the significance of where we are."

"We're in New York in the crown of the Statue of Liberty. Isn't it obvious?"

"Do you understand the meaning of liberty?"

"Not here, Nora." She moves away from me and uses others to create distance between us.

Once we descend the stairs and walk out of the pedestal and stand a short distance away, I find myself looking back up, and while recalling Auguste's phrase, I shout, "Viva liberty!"

"Nora! You're embarrassing me."

"How so?" I demand.

"There are people around us, don't you see?"

"Yes. And I wonder if they have a better appreciation for this great lady than you."

"I don't know what you're talking about. Maybe we should go back now."

"Here is a sign, Ella, a sign that we have a more rewarding destiny awaiting us rather than the conventional."

"Good gracious, Nora! I am not so liberated to forsake the conventional. I declare, your notions have evolved quite dramatically since arriving in New York."

"Not at all, Ella. They have been a part of my deepest desires for years but are only revealed to me since we have come here."

"That's all well and good for you, Nora, but I am content with the … what would you call it?"

"The ordinary life."

"Yes. Fine. I am perfectly willing to live an ordinary life made from the usual conventions of ordinary."

"And so you will go back to where we came from, marry Soren, bear his children, and never think of what could have been?"

"Nora, this was your dream. Not mine. I'm here only because you are here."

"So I suspected." I'm ready to kick the nearest park bench.

"What are you talking about now?" Her voice sounds like my mother's scolding.

"So you only came along in hopes of finding something better."

"What a conclusion to jump to."

I'm not sure if I'm having a moment of lucidity or merely a tantrum, so I stop the conversation abruptly. I cannot explain to Ella the nature of my true feelings as I am no longer quite sure of them myself.

I sit down on a bench, its back less comfortable than I imagined. Sighing with despair, I now watch Ella remove the chain given to her from her grandmother.

"Here, Nora." She holds it out, the emblem dangling, ready to deposit in my hand, which I have kept deliberately unavailable. "In the spirit of our long-term friendship, I think my grandmother would have wanted this to go to someone who was intent on becoming a bona-fide nurse. Take it as a symbol of our deep friendship."

"No, thank you," I say curtly. "I am probably less likely to become a nurse than you are. I suddenly find I have other interests as well."

"What do you mean?"

"Never mind." I look far off at nothing in particular.

We say not a word on the ferry ride back or on the trolley ride down Broadway. As we walk back to the boardinghouse, it begins to dawn on both of us that we are lost.

"Ella, I think we have walked too far."

"I think we got off at the wrong stop."

Ella is right. I do not recognize this part of the city. Just as we come upon the next corner, a man and woman appear before us. I stop short of running into the woman while Ella steps behind me so as to avoid colliding with the man.

The woman's hair, dark and unkempt, weaves treachery while the darkness behind her toothless grin gives me shivers. Her soiled and tattered dress is more like an old discarded table cloth revealing her bare arms and bust line.

"What have we here?" she asks, her breath smelling of spirits.

The man walks behind me while Ella backs up against me and begins reaching for my hand. "A pair of fancies from up Harlem way be my wager," I hear the man say with a leering tone.

"More like a couple of tarts from the Points." The woman looks me straight in the eye. "Lost your way, missy?"

"I guess you could say that." I am forcing a smile while, at the same time, my forehead becomes damp with perspiration.

"Ha!" she interrupts, snapping like a viper. "More like a couple of rubes. You two is way off track, ain't ya?"

"Yes. We're from out west. Minnesota."

"Minnesota?" the man ponders. I turn to see that he is of good size and dressed no better than his companion. "What country is that?"

"It's … a … state," says Ella. I can feel her terror by way of her tight grip on my hand."

"Blimey, Herc. What do you care? You don't know the difference 'tween the two anyhow."

"'Course I does, Collie, you two-bit whore. My old man died in the Battle 'tween the States, so I guess I know somethin' about it." I watch him scowl at the woman and then he looks Ella up and down. "Hey, you're a pretty thing," he says to Ella.

"Th … thank you."

And now he looks at me. "You're friend ain't too bad lookin' none."

"You two should meet Holder," the woman suggests. "He's always looking for new talent."

"Is he your employer?" I ask.

Both the man and woman laugh. "Yeah, you could say that."

Only a few windows here and there in the nearby buildings shine with light, but even so, they are quite dim. The corner street lamp is out. The lack of good lighting merely accentuates our predicament.

"Why don't you two come along with us?" The woman takes me by the elbow.

"Perhaps another time," I begin to say, "as we're really quite late. Mrs. Gorman expects all her young ladies in by ten o'clock."

"You *ladies* need to come with us." The man takes Ella's arm and pulls her close to him. "Holder would be unforgiving if he knew I let you two fine things slip through my fingers."

I look around, wanting to shout, but realize *who would hear?* Certainly a tenant in one of the buildings would. I pull Ella close to me as we are directed farther down the street.

Just as I am about to scream, the man whispers, "Not a peep out of either of you."

We make our way through a labyrinth of streets, and I am sure I am losing track of where we've been. It hardly seems to matter, as we were lost from the start. Our pace is slow yet deliberate, which I attribute to the gait of Herc, who is dragging a game leg.

"Are you injured, dear sir?" I attempt to appeal to his better nature, hoping to reach a kind spot in his heart, if such a place exists.

"Never you mind. I'm quite all right."

"He ain't hurt. He got himself crippled up for foulin' up a job."

"Shut your hole, woman, or I'll shut it for ya."

"It's just that," I stammer, "we're trained nurses and would be most willing to help you."

"I say you never mind. We'll get you on nursing duty before too long." He laughs, and Collie begins to laugh as well.

The alleyways darken with each side street we cross. It feels as though we are descending a mineshaft.

The sides of windowless walls reaching high above are streaked with water stains, and the dank odor of mold and refuse grows stronger. I begin to imagine we are below ground, lowered into a grave.

I know we are running out of time; something has to be done. As we clear the next side street, I find myself instinctively pulling away from Ella and using her body to block the reach of Herc. I am able to break free, like a screen door with a resilient spring. I run back up the alleyway as fast as I my laced boots will carry me, panicked, thinking of my home so far away.

"Get back here!" The man's voice is as large as he. I can hear his sloth-like pace decreasing in volume.

"You get back here, you big ape!" The woman sounds angrier than before. "Help me with this troublesome wench!"

As I step into the street, I hear an unrecognizable scream back far off in the darkness. "Nora!"

I stop and think about going back but determine there is no point to it. I need to find help. Could I do it without running into more of the same trouble?

I make my way toward the lights of the city and away from the shadows and darkness where I left Ella behind.

Finally, I am standing on a street not so crowded but at least with people who appear to be of my own kind. I look for a constable. There is usually one to be found on every street corner during the day, but it's late, and I have to run up and down several more streets before spotting one.

I approach him, exhausted. "Help," I gasp while grabbing the constable by the arm.

"What's this?" he asks, startled by my nearly tearing off the sleeve of his uniform.

"I need help. My friend has been kidnapped."

"Calm yourself first, lass." His face looks kind with smiling eyes beneath his hat and a mustache, evenly cut, revealing a lower lip hanging with concern. "Now what's all this about a kidnapping?"

I explain the situation, but instead of running with me back to where I had come from, he says, "I'm sorry, miss, but you'll have to report this to the precinct. There's one just up the street about two blocks."

I look to where he points. "And you're sure that someone there will be quick to help me find my friend?"

"You can see the front of the building just beneath that group of lights. Allow me to escort you."

"Thank you." My legs are now less shaky as my heart beats slower.

"I'm sorry, Ms. Thorsen," says the officer behind the desk, "but the part of the city you're describing is not within our precinct. I can send word over to the proper authorities to make them aware of your friend's situation, but, I'm afraid, it is quite an undertaking for such a large city."

"But everyone needs to act now, don't you see? While the trail is still warm."

"I'm sorry, miss, but the city just doesn't have the manpower to conduct such an undertaking. The city has hundreds of cases every year of people gone missing, even some of their own volition."

I have no doubt my look of disapproval for the officer's insinuation is registering. But his attempt to provide assurance by way of a weak, empty smile does not. He then concludes by claiming, "I'm sure the precinct in question will assign investigators to the case as soon as tomorrow morning."

"But the longer it takes, the less likely Ella will be found."

"Our hands are tied here, miss. Best you can do is to go home and try to get some rest. I'll have one of our officers drive you."

As I ride with the escorting officer, I think about how recklessly I have deserted Ella, and now, desperately, I try to imagine how I can help her. Whose help could I solicit?

"What's the address?" asks the officer.

Without hesitating, almost subconsciously, I blurt out Monsieur Valadon's address. "Three forty Varick."

I find Auguste awake.

"What brings you out this way so late at night, Nora?" He takes my hands in his and leads me upstairs to his residence.

"The most terrible of circumstances." I am trembling and on the verge of sobbing as I explain from start to finish.

"This is an unfortunate business, indeed. I should like to help you in any way I can, but I am not very familiar with the part of the city you describe. Can you think of anyone else's help we could solicit?"

I think of Tristan and Soren. They have lived in the city for a number of years. Surely, I believe, they would be able to help.

As we make our way back across the city through many more streets, I think of Ella's plight and how not only her captors are the enemy but time as well.

"And you've notified the proper authorities?" asks Soren, slowly rubbing a closed fist in the palm of his other hand while displaying an edginess I had not previously witnessed.

"I already told you I had, and I was told there is nothing to be done until the morning."

"What!" His eyes, dark pools of anger, betray a temper seething beneath his otherwise passive disposition.

"Be calm, Soren," says Tristan, placing a sturdy hand upon his friend's shoulder.

"My betrothed has been abducted by the vilest elements of the city, and you expect me to be calm?"

"Please, Soren," begs Auguste with both patience and reason. "Would it not be best if we conducted our own search right now rather than standing here debating the matter?"

⚜

I now feel we are in the exact spot where Ella and I encountered Herc and Collie.

"Are you sure, my dear?" asks Auguste, tapping his cane against the lamp post.

"Yes. I recall this unlit street lamp and the scratches on this side of the pole that resemble a W."

"So where should we go from here, Nora?" Tristan's voice is calm as he places a gentle hand on my forearm.

I quickly look in all directions, shuffling my memories like a deck of cards, expecting the Queen of Hearts to appear, happy and safe. "It was down this street," I say with cautious certainty.

We rush down several backstreets and alleys until everything—lampposts and tenement stoops—begins to look the same all over again. And just as we are about to give up hope, Soren spots a crumpled figure, huddled in the darkness, quite near where I had abandoned Ella.

When we come upon Ella, she appears to be unconscious. As I step forward, I can hear her sobbing and pleading. "No more," she says, over and over.

"Ella," I whisper. "My dear Ella." My voice begins to crack with the sound of her name. I kneel on the ground and gather her to me.

"You left me, Nora." She looks at my face, her eyes sunken, filled with despair. "You left me all alone."

Just then, we hear footsteps approaching from the end of the alleyway, one of which sounds like the dragging foot of Herc.

"Good evening, gents," says a stranger, appearing smartly dressed. "My young lady seems to have wandered off."

"That's the other one, boss," I hear Herc mumble.

"I'm her friend," I say, overcome by a surge of both anger and shame. I press Ella to me tightly. I close my eyes even tighter, but the tears of shame burst through.

Then I hear Soren shouting, "Filthy vermin!" And as I look up, I see him take from Auguste his cane and, without pausing even for a moment, strike the well-dressed man across the face, felling him into a nearby pile of refuse.

Herc begins to rush Soren, but both Tristan and Auguste intercept his advance. Tristan grabs for Herc's head while Auguste throws himself into his bad leg. Now he moans in pain as both men pin him to the ground.

Soren is about to strike the man again when I hear someone shout from up the alleyway, "Hey, you lot! What's the idea?"

The man lying in the garbage lifts himself out. As he stands, he stammers, "Arrest this man, Malloy, for assault."

"Is that you, Holder?" asks the officer. "What kind of trouble is brewing here? Let that man up." Tristan and Auguste cautiously get off Herc and step away.

Soren levels the cane at Holder as his whole body begins to relax. "I'd like to report a kidnapping, Constable," he demands.

"And I'd…like to…report an assault." Holder sounds woozy as he tries to maintain his balance by reaching for the wall.

"Shut up, you!" shouts Soren, "Or I'll give you another crack!"

"You stand down, young man," snaps the constable, pointing his billy club at Soren, "and drop that weapon at your feet. Now who can tell me what is going on here?"

"This man kidnapped this woman and exposed her to unthinkable acts of cruelty," says Soren.

"You just remember, Malloy, who puts brass in your pocket," says Holder.

The constable raises his hands to calm everyone down as I help Ella to her feet. "Now let's everyone take it easy." He looks at Soren. "Sir, how can you report a kidnapping when the person you say is kidnapped is standing right in front of you?" His smile is out of place.

Tristan looks first at Ella and me. Then, turning to the constable, and with a very discretionary tone, he begins to speak. "It's by sheer luck we came upon her lying here in the alley. I think, sir, you should consider the facts more carefully."

"And you'll not suggest to me how to do my business, sir, or I'll be forced to run you in." Then he places the tip of his billy club on Tristan's chest and shoves him back a pace. "Now then, as I say, there is no one missing, so there is no crime."

"I'm bleeding here, Malloy," says Holder. "I want something done with this one." He points to Soren.

"I think, Holder, the best thing is to let this business settle for the night. Don't you agree?"

Holder looks at Malloy and then to us. "I don't want to see you lot around here again. You understand?"

"All right, you three shove off. I'll see the ladies home."

"We can conduct these ladies home," says Auguste.

"It's my duty. I aim to carry it through." He looks to all the men, evidently waiting for any and all to posture up to his authority, should they dare. "So I say again, you gentlemen can be on your way. Unless, of course, you prefer the company of the evening's collection of derelicts gathered in the wagon up the street. Your choice."

Tristan approaches Ella and me. "Don't worry. We'll follow close behind."

Ella and I sit up front with Constable Malloy as he steers us slowly toward our boardinghouse. There are the occasional sounds of cries and shouts from the back of the wagon.

He speaks, but I am not interested in conversing with him. "It's a mystery in this world how things like this happen. I think it's mostly carelessness that leads to such things. I guess it's best to just look upon it as a lesson learned and leave it at that."

Mrs. Gorman sees the constable accompanying us as she opens the door. The look on her face tells me we will not be harangued for our tardiness.

"Come with me, girl." She takes Ella by the arm.

As Ella and Mrs. Gorman disappear inside, the constable takes me by my elbow. "You'll know next time, miss. Am I right?"

"Of course, Constable," I respond. "And no doubt, God willing, you'll remember all your life the part you played this very night."

Tristan and Malloy cross paths on the steps.

"I'm so sorry, Nora," he begins, "about all the trouble you've endured this evening. I wish to convey my most humble apologies on behalf of this fair city."

"It's not your place, Tristan, but I do appreciate your concern and your help." I smile.

"Well, you're both safe and sound now."

"Yes. We're home." I know we are safe, but we are not sound. "Thank you for all your help and your friendship. It is far more valuable than I can express. Would you please thank Soren and Auguste on my behalf as well?"

"Of course. Well, good night, Nora."

"Good night." I wave to the others. Soren sits sullen while Auguste tips his cane toward me.

After a long, hot bath, I take Ella to our room. I sit her down on her bed. She moves to rest against the headboard. She sits there looking straight off into an abyss.

I can see the change that has come over Ella. She is no longer as I remember her just from this morning. She appears young, so much younger than her eighteen years. She is like a lost little girl, only now devastated from the imbalance of a world where the weak are preyed upon, the sick cast aside, and the powerful hold no regard.

I can feel that I had changed as well. I feel much older. I am less tolerant. I am beginning to boil within. I can feel Ella's pain inside me. This is not part of my plan. We were riding the world like two kindred souls, together on a Ferris wheel.

I turn out the light and say good night to Ella. She doesn't respond.

*October 1899*

Ella sits most days as though she is in a trance. Our conversations are stilted and often about the past and "back home." I struggle to help her find interest in our surroundings or our studies. A conversation repeats itself.

*"When can we go home, Nora?"*

*"Whenever you want. I can secure us passage three days hence, if you like."*

*"No. I've changed my mind. That's too soon. I don't think we should go just yet."*

*"Why not? How is it too soon?"*

*"I don't know. I'm just not ready."*

I lie to her about how much we are enjoying our new life.

I suspect the lies I write home will surely compound over time. I have already, immediately after our experience, written to Ella's parents regarding her change of mind in returning home. I lied that Ella was experiencing a bout of fever but had been taken well in hand by the local hospital and no one should worry over her condition. She forbade me from telling the truth, binding my words tighter to a litany of lies. How could I explain future correspondence that would also be written in my hand and voice?

A part of me knows I should take Ella firmly in hand, whisking her away back to Minnesota. But the larger part of me, the selfish part, is content to bide its time as it waits patiently for Ella to snap out of that which has overtaken her mind and body.

⚜

The parlor of Tristan and Soren's rented brownstone is well kept by a maid who is unavailable today. Desperate, I am beyond risking impropriety by begging both their admittance and guidance.

"This is a tricky business," Tristan explains while clumsily handing me a cup of tea. "From what I can gather, Ella has had a traumatic experience which has had untold affect on her mind."

"I don't understand why she won't talk about these things." I rub my temples and sigh in frustration.

"It's possible," Soren says, "that she is repressing her thoughts and emotions to protect herself from experiencing her pain externally. I can't explain it very well. I am just now aware of studies being conducted in Europe regarding such things."

"This is true," Tristan adds. "It is referred to as psychoanalysis."

"Very heady business," I lament. "But hardly useful at this point in time, unless either of you gentlemen can prescribe a remedy."

"Not in the way of a physical medication," Tristan responds. "But rather a verbal prescription, which neither myself nor, if I may say so, Soren are qualified to administer."

"My recommendation," says Soren, "is you return her post haste to her family back in Minnesota."

"She does not want to return home," I hiss. Soren straightens in his chair for a moment but then nods and waves off my statement.

With calm reason, Tristan now makes his point heard. "Perhaps it is no longer her place to decide."

I ignore Tristan and, instead, continue to direct my anger at Soren. "And what is your position to your betrothed?" I ask with firm disapproval. "I sense all at once a breach in your engagement."

"These were intentions," Soren explains, "on which Ella and I had ruminated. We had not gone so far as to receive parental approval. As you well know, she was to return home to surprise her parents with our news, to feel them out regarding her decision to forego an education. And under the circumstances, an announcement of engagement at this point would only further complicate things. Surely, you can see that, Nora."

"I do." I slouch, imperceptibly, to mull over the circumstances. "The dictates of men in a man's world. How profoundly cruel."

"Now, Nora." Tristan leans toward me. "Be reasonable."

"At any rate, I don't know how any of that matters." I straighten my posture. "You've called on her nary once since the incident."

"Busy." He shifts in his chair while I wait for him to spew more words less convincing than the first. "Time of year. Obligations."

"Obligations, indeed. Such a luxury to pick and choose those you should follow through on."

Soren makes no effort for restraint and bolts upright. "Don't imagine you can exclude yourself from blame in any of this." He points an accusatory finger at me as easily as he had pointed Auguste's cane at the ne'er do well some months ago. "Ella told me long ago how controlling you can be. Even I felt as though she and I needed to tip-toe around you regarding our intimacy."

I am not so timid and quickly rise while gently setting my cup and saucer on the nearby table. "This conversation can no longer continue." I look to Tristan. "Thank you for your past friendship, but under the current circumstances, I think it would be best if we were not to see one another in the future."

"Are you sure, Nora?" Tristan appears crestfallen as he stands to intercept my rush for the front door.

"I'm afraid so." I can't look him in the eyes. I know what my obligations are, and I intend to carry them out. "I'm truly sorry."

❧

*December 1899*

Auguste has graciously invited Ella and me to the opening of a musical playing on Broadway. I'm hoping to use the occasion as a diversion to help lift Ella's spirits. The past several weeks have been discomforting for me as I try endlessly to persuade Ella to excel in her studies and to enjoy the benefits of living in the city.

"We've been in the city for months, Ella, and have yet to see a show. Aren't you excited by the invitation?"

"Yes. That would be nice." Her response lacks enthusiasm but, instead, is as cold and gray as the December sky. I refuse to allow her to ruin the long Christmas week vacation. And now I remember Ella owes her parents a letter. I intend to forge one to them soon, I promise myself. Will my worries never end?

Auguste drives us to the Third Avenue Theatre through the chilly night air. He attempts to engage Ella in conversation. She is polite, though reticent.

"Aside from Christmas programs performed by our church back home," she explains, "I have attended only a small number of plays."

"But not, certainly, as grand a venue as the one to which we are on our way."

"I'm sure you are right, Auguste. Both Ella and I are very grateful for your invitation."

The theatre is as grand as any church in the neighborhood. The walls are painted red and salmon and are streaked with bronze and blue. The ceiling is high above our balcony seats. I need to lean forward to see the people seated below, which I don't do, as I am feeling giddy and a bit of a snob this evening. I anticipate the opening of the red satin curtain hanging from the proscenium arch, which sits upon the stage in nearly a full circle.

The title of the musical is *A Trip to Coontown*. Auguste tells us all the actors, managers, and musicians are made up entirely of blacks. This explanation lends to the reasoning why there are so many black people in the crowd.

I have never been among so many people of color and begin to ponder my impression of the surroundings. I remember very few times, while growing up, when I had the occasion to engage people not of my own race. But suddenly I have this overwhelming appreciation for other races as being equal to my own. Though I had never thought of them as less, I realize now that I had never given this notion consideration at all.

As the music begins, I notice Ella appears engaged, and I have a feeling of peace and easiness I have not felt in months. I convince myself this is just the medicine she needs to bring her out of herself.

The musical tells of a con man attempting to fleece an elderly black man out of his old-age pension. A number of the musical scores are catchy, and the story is humorous at times. It is easy for me to join the crowd in the joy of being lost in a story that is not told in book form.

❧

The evening has been so pleasant. Even the chilly ride back felt as refreshing as a Minnesota hayride under moonlight. Auguste saw both Ella and I to the door. I gave him a warm embrace.

"A wonderful show," I say to Mrs. Gorman while ascending the stairs. She is but another kind soul who had waited up for our safe return. Her unpinned hair lies heavy against the cozy red and green robe Ella and I gave her for Christmas.

I rush to open the window to capture one last breath of the evening air. "Hasn't it been a wonderful evening, Ella?" She mutters something inaudible, and I turn to see her lost in the bad mood that has moved in with us.

"Ella," I begin, "I want very much to help you, but you need to talk to me. You need to explain what is ailing you."

"I just wish we could go home, Nora. Do you remember the picnics our families shared down by the Red River every Fourth of July?"

"You know I do, Ella. But this is not July, and we are nowhere near the Red River. It is two days before the new century. And we are here in the most exciting city in the world."

"Do you remember the New Year's Eve celebrations we shared back home?"

"Of course, I do. You know I remember those as well."

"We would gather at the church and help decorate for the evening's festivities."

"I seem to recall most New Year's evenings as very cold. And some even with snowfall."

"But we didn't mind."

"I think I minded walking through all the snow." I try to share a smile with Ella.

"How white the snow was."

"Yes."

"Pure."

"Yes, Ella."

"The snow was so pure. The air was cold, but it was clean."

"Yes, my dear. Those are good memories to have."

"But you see, Nora, I'm no longer pure. I'm no longer clean."

"Nonsense, Ella. You're the same good friend I've known all my life. There's nothing changed about you. You've just had a bad experience that you need to put behind you. You need to think of all the new and exciting experiences you and I are going to share between now and the time we're rocking side by side on some beautiful porch overlooking the most beautiful fields with the most beautiful trees and the most beautiful sky above."

"That sounds nice, Nora, very nice."

"Yes, Ella, it will be nice."

Just then Ella's eyes go blank, staring far off. Back to Minnesota, I imagine. She lets out a slow, quiet sigh, and says, "I'll find my own Red River."

I can no longer understand Ella. It is as if the bond between us has changed into a bridge made of willow, tenuous and abysmal. I now make a New Year's resolution. I shall resign myself to taking Ella back to Minnesota after the holidays have ended. To secure passage now would be both chaotic and costly.

All else must be placed on hold as I convince myself that dreams may be fleeting but they have their place as much as the realities of life.

I touch Ella's shoulder to stir her back from far off. "Ella?" She turns her head and stares, almost catatonic. "I know the holidays are nearly past, but I think I'd like to return to Minnesota for a little visit. Would you care to join me?"

"Home?"

"Yes. Home. Would you like that?"

She slowly shakes her head, and her eyes grow large. "No, Nora. I can't go home."

Suddenly, I'm scared for the future. How foolish I've been for not truly considering how far Ella has fallen into despair.

"You don't have to decide now." I smile through my sadness and flick her soft bangs. "Just think about it."

❧

The first thing I see New Year's Eve day is Ella's empty, unmade bed, and then I notice the door to our room ajar.

Downstairs during breakfast, I quietly ask Mrs. Gorman if she noticed Ella leaving the boardinghouse early this morning.

"No. I did not see her, but I would surely have stopped her from leaving the premises so early under the cover of darkness."

I return to Ella's and my room to look through her things and discover that nothing is missing. All of her outer clothing is still here. Every stitch. Good God! What is she wearing? I rush outside to the street, looking in both directions. My heart is racing like a frightened rabbit, and my eyes are starving for a glimpse of Ella. I think of places she might be. Places we have frequented. It's Sunday. The library will be closed. And what other places will be closed since it is the day before the New Year? No matter. I must look. I must.

I spend all day wandering the streets, entering an endless number of establishments. I even consider the notion to walk through the dark alleyways where Ella and I were once lost, imagining she has been kidnapped during the previous night. But I know this is foolish thinking. I remember what she told me the night before. I empty my head of the gravity of her words.

I am barely able to sleep New Year's Eve night while anticipating Ella's return. But it is not to be. The revelers continue long into the night. This is a new experience, that of much celebration in the face of tragedy. I guess they're all too busy with their own lives to bother themselves with my plight. Everyone is sharing the beginning of the new century except me. I am alone in the most crowded city in the world.

New Year's morning, I awake to pounding hooves and the grinding of rolling wooden wheels against the frozen gravel street. I wash my face with the cool water from the basin and dress, only to sit motionless, staring out the window to the street below.

As I open the window, Mrs. Gorman's tomcat startles me as he jumps in from the fire escape. He is purring, not a care in the world, and begins to rub against my kneecaps. He twists and turns back and forth while I reflect on the poor choices I made over the past months.

❧

"Could you describe the state of mind of your friend on the day she disappeared?" The precinct detective's desk is cluttered like his face, unshaven and eyebrows askew. The top of his thick, brown hair lies to the right in some places and to the left or straight up in others.

"She was the same as she had been for the past several weeks."

"And how was that?"

"Distant. Despondent."

"Do you know why?"

"She had been…" I try to find the right words. "Misused by very evil people."

"In what way?"

"In what way? Sir, I am telling you what I know."

"But what you're saying is that…" He pauses to review the report. "Your friend had been violated. And you believe this to be the cause of her state of mind since then 'til her disappearance?"

"Yes."

The investigator leans forward and lowers his voice, asking me, "I don't wish to be indelicate, Ms. Thorsen, but are you familiar with the term *suicide*?"

I stare into the man's face as I begin to contemplate his implication that my Ella has committed suicide. "Of course, I am familiar with the term. It is the greatest sin someone can commit against God."

"I'm not so concerned about the morality of such an occurrence but more so the likelihood that a person might feel compelled to take such an action."

"You're quite mistaken, sir. Both my friend and I come from a strong Lutheran upbringing, and there is no conceivable reason for which she would ever consider such an act."

"I can't speak for the heart and mind of an individual. I bring up the subject for you to consider. The city is filled with people of varying degrees of suffering. Some choose to relieve their suffering by taking their own lives. We have several cases each year of such incidents, a number of which jump into the river."

"I can't accept your theory, sir. I believe she is alive, and I intend to find her in this cesspool you call a city." But even as I say this, I remember Ella's last words about finding her own Red River. I go over in my mind Ella's and my final conversation. Surely she was pleading with me to take her home, back to Minnesota.

Another difficult task lay before me. How does one notify the parents of a dear friend to inform them their daughter is missing? *You just write it, you silly fool, truthfully, and you bear and live with knowing that you are undeniably responsible.* No. That won't do. A telegraph. I will send a telegraph instead. One appealing for help. But whom to send it to? Not Ella's parents. That would be too cruel for them to learn about it in such an impersonal way. My eldest brother, Trygg. He is resourceful and can be counted upon.

> *Trygg Thorsen, Thief River Falls, MN*
> *Urgent! Please come at once. Appeal your discretion.*
> *Nora*

⁕

Trygg arrives today, three days since I sent the telegraph. I spent those three days searching for Ella. My methods were limited. I spent most days wandering the streets, looking at every face I passed. But now that Trygg is coming, we can begin a more fruitful search, I'm certain.

"I am so grateful you are here, Trygg," I say, embracing him as he steps off the train.

"Nora. You have put me in a very difficult position both with my employer and with our parents."

I start to cry from my relief at the presence of someone from back home.

"I'm sorry that I am short with you … " He takes me by my shoulders and moves me to arms' length, staring into my face. "What is it, dear sister? What has happened to you?"

"Not me," I begin, sobbing. "Ella."

"Ella? All right. What has happened to Ella?"

"She is missing."

"Missing?" His clean-shaven face brings out the seriousness in his voice. "How? Why?"

"It's a long story. We should go somewhere out of the cold, but I'm not sure where."

"Can't we go back to your room?"

"No!"

"Why not there?"

"I've not mentioned Ella's disappearance to the landlady just yet."

Trygg spins me around again to face him. "Stupid girl! What are you playing at?"

"Not here," I plead.

"But surely, she is suspicious of Ella's absence?"

"I told her she has returned to Minnesota on extended leave."

"Equally suspicious, no doubt."

We make our way back to a nearby beer garden, where Trygg orders two coffees. I explain the circumstances from first to last regarding Ella's disappearance. My brother grows impatient with my self-deprecating account.

"Nora! Stop blaming yourself. Ella, like you, knew what she was getting into when she came out East. I think it does nothing to improve Ella's lot when you focus all your attention on how her disappearance has impacted you. Do you understand?"

He reaches across the table and takes my hand in his and then smiles. I smile in return and nod. "But I promised her parents I would look after her."

"Did you really? Did you really promise?" His eyes remind me of the truth. Nothing said, perhaps, but just as strong a commitment is that not spoken. "Even if you had, I don't think that is a promise they would truly intend for you to keep. But I'm sure you did the best you could."

But I had a multitude of secrets I could not bear to share with Trygg. I could not stop thinking about my selfishness.

"So the police are of no service?" asks Trygg.

"They are few in number, and their business, they assure me, is quite overwhelming."

"And these gentlemen you are acquainted with?"

"Both Tristan and Soren are busy with their academics, and Auguste has limited knowledge of the city."

Now my brother speaks of mother and father and our brothers and sisters. He assures me everyone is quite well. He also asks me to consider returning to Minnesota with him. "I realize, Nora, you have a zest for life, but due to this business with Ella, shouldn't you consider returning home?"

"How, dear brother, could you ask me to do such a thing?"

"I've known you all my life, Nora. I know how you persevere. But sometimes you do so in vain."

"I don't know what you're talking about."

"Remember the old tree limb."

"Of course, I do. It failed me."

"Did it? Don't you remember how we would always climb that big cedar near the house, everyone taking their places?"

"You always had to be on the top branch, I seem to recall."

"Yes. But only until I learned that it was too weak to hold my weight. So too was it with the branch you climbed to just below me. I was wise enough to stop climbing so high. But you insisted on climbing to that branch long after you should have known better."

"I recall not breaking my neck in the end."

"Yes. That was very fortunate for us all. But my point is that you may be doing the same thing here in New York. You need to consider what you are capable of handling."

"I have much to do before I can return home, Trygg."

"All right, but please consider it."

"I never considered the climbing of trees to be exclusive to boys. Nor do I think the world to be exclusive to men."

"Same old stubborn Nora." Trygg leans back in his chair, shaking his head. "There's something in what you say, dear sister, but I can't help but think you are years ahead of your time in your thinking."

<hr />

I am alone again in New York. A week after his arrival, Trygg has left, as we have exhausted our efforts and resources in searching for Ella. I can no longer keep him from his obligations back home. He is a good brother, and I am thankful for all his help and advice. But there are things that must remain unspoken. I sent a sealed letter with him to be delivered to Ella's parents. I wrote it the previous evening while coming to terms with what I had done.

*Dear Mr. and Mrs. Pederson,*

*It is with great sorrow that I write to you regarding the disappearance of your daughter and my dearest friend, Ella. My brother, Trygg, has agreed to answer any and all of your questions as it would be far too difficult for me to put down here in words.*

*For my part, I wish to express the joys and experiences Ella and I shared while residing in New York City, as well as our time growing up together. I could not have asked for a better companion to accompany me anywhere in the world or a better friend to grow alongside. As you know, she and I were inseparable and, truth be told, I truly believe she was the better part of me with her innocence and trust in others.*

*Unfortunately, I feel I have broken your trust by not taking care of Ella all the months we have been here together. I cannot express in words the shame or the guilt I now feel for betraying your trust. I know it is much to ask, but in the name of God, I beg your forgiveness.*

*With my deepest regrets,*
*Nora*

Nearly a month has passed since Ella's disappearance. Every day, I walk to each of the nearby precincts, and every day, each one provides the same information. No leads. No reports. And each day I feel as though I am in a city that is too large to manage its affairs, too large to keep track of its citizens. If there is a benefit to the existence of large cities, it escapes me. Of course, I know this is my own bitterness. I am merely blaming exterior sources to avoid my own culpability. *Mea culpa*. I am to blame. I have allowed my selfishness, my need for Ella to always be near … to at once cause me to lose someone so important to me. *Mea culpa*: a silly Latin phrase with a very powerful meaning. And now it is my cross to bear. My faith is now being tested. And my fear of death ignited by my own desire to be dead. Perhaps it is a simple matter after all to become so filled with despair that taking one's own life becomes a credible alternative.

*And why*, I ask myself. *What is the reason Ella had lived and died, if she is, in fact, lost forever?* It makes no sense. I feel as though the entire world has been ripped out from under me. The concept of God lies bare before me. I can't understand his notion of life and death. I try to think of Ella in His heaven, but the thought does not take.

# I Am Lonely

Turn to me and be gracious to me for I am
lonely and afflicted. The troubles of my heart
have multiplied; free me from my anguish.

Psalm 25: 16–17

I need an out. I am beginning to lose my bearings. I
can no longer endure this city and the circumstances
that have brought me to this point. I am remiss in my
studies. I have long since parted ways with Tristan, in
spite of the tragic experience we shared back in New
Richmond. I know it is unfair, but I consider him
guilty by association with Soren.

Auguste's company, I find necessary. Both his adora-
tion for me and my fondness for him provide equilib-
rium; although, at times, I pause when confronted with
his openness regarding so many subjects. The best way
to describe his worldliness: ambiguous and tolerant.

I find it difficult to look at Auguste's portrait of
Ella and me. I now see the two figures in the painting
in an entirely different light. I appear overly dominant,
while Ella has a submissive look about her.

"Nora, I understand the pain you are going through."
Auguste's empathy is evident in his soft eyes. "God
knows the dead of winter is nowhere to find oneself
with such raw emotions."

I feign a positive demeanor, chin up and lithe in
step, as I move about his studio. "Oh, Auguste. This

winter has been tame compared to those I experienced growing up. Minnesota is quite a cold place in the winter time."

He smiles, pausing to absorb my observation. And then his expression turns serious, as though he has something weighing on his conscience.

"My dear, I fear you will find me both forward and presumptuous but..." He pauses.

"Yes, Auguste?"

"How would you feel about sharing the springtime with me back in my beloved Paris?"

I let his question sink in. I am quite enamored by the notion of going farther east, imagining I would be leaving my burden in my wake.

"My heart aches knowing you would be left here all alone to fend for yourself."

I should instantly rebuff such a proposal, but I find myself absorbed by this very notion.

"Of course, there would be no question of impropriety. I have at my disposal a quiet little apartment that you could have all to yourself."

"But how could I pay you the rent, Auguste?"

"That would be no concern of yours. You would be my guest."

"It is most generous, but I feel I would become a burden upon you."

"Not at all. Perhaps as a way of appreciation, you would allow me to paint your likeness in numerous settings."

"I couldn't expect you to spend your days painting me, though it's quite flattering. I would need to occupy myself with useful endeavors."

"I'm sure you could do volunteer nursing at any of the nearby hospitals. And besides, there would be many activities for us to partake in."

"You must make me one promise, Auguste."

"What is that, Nora?"

"Please store this portrait away. I would prefer to never set eyes upon it ever again."

"It will be done." He lifts the painting high in the air and then spins it round and sets it down facing against the wall. "And *you* must promise me one thing."

"Yes?"

"You will consider partaking in that which Paris offers the most of."

"Which is?"

"The perpetual birth and flow of love."

I begin to blush. "Dear, dear Auguste."

Sensing my embarrassment, he lightens the moment. "But at the very least, you must help me to enjoy the *Exposition Universelle*."

❦

*March 1900*

If I felt out of place on first arrival to New York, the feeling is tenfold in Paris. I attribute this feeling to the steady influx and ubiquitous presence of so many foreigners gathering for the World's Fair. Auguste has the patience of Job as he teaches me the French language, but I still find myself stumbling through simple conversations with the odd acquaintance.

The local hospital is more than willing to allow me to do volunteer work, although my duties are quite lim-

ited due to my lack of practical nursing skills and igno-
rance of French. I resolve to attend the university to learn
the native language, as well as to take instruction in the
philosophical sciences Tristan spoke of last summer.
Admittedly, my interest in such things has piqued as I
feel abandoned by my own religious beliefs. Perhaps life
isn't as simple as I had always imagined. In the meantime,
I will choose to set aside my childhood dreams and aspi-
rations, if not empty my head of them entirely.

I feel foolish. I lament from my silly notion that life
could travel so smoothly, without disruption. Why did
I ever think that I could march through the world—
Ella by my side—playing the part, say, of a doctor, or
even an owner of a business of some kind, particularly
in a man's world?

❦

On weekends, during the course of spring turning into
summer, Auguste and I attend various local events,
including yacht races and horse shows.

Today is the *Prix Exbury*, and Auguste and I are in
Saint Cloud, near Paris. The mid-March air is refreshing as we stroll arm-in-arm under a calm, blue sky.
It feels good to be away from the disorganization of
Montmartre. The confusion created by vendors and
artists populating the streets adds to my burden of
feeling out of place. But here, at the racecourse, I feel
less so. And I'm beginning to find comfort in casual
conversation with the locals.

"These are the finest thoroughbreds from all
round," Auguste explains. "Keep your eyes on number

twelve, Fourire, as he is the defending champion. A good friend of mine, whom we shall meet after the race, has part stake in the beast."

But my mind is elsewhere as I watch the horses round the first turn. The name of the racecourse, Saint Cloud, reminds me of the town of Saint Cloud in Minnesota. And this merely transports me back to my own rural home. And once again, I am thinking of Ella. She is like a saint named Cloud. She is like a cloud hanging over me.

I contemplate God as the racers break down the backstretch. He has followed me across the Atlantic, I now realize. I need to come to terms with my faith, of which I have been remiss since the loss of Ella.

"Know who you are, Daughter," my father had bellowed, like God to Moses, just before my departure.

"If I knew that," I had said with tears, "I should think I would not have cause to leave." I now long for his firm and comforting embrace that has been packed away since.

"Here he comes!" Auguste shouts. "From the outside!"

I smile at Auguste, delighted with his joy. He is an aging soul who has his own crosses to bear but does so with a zest unburdened by such things as faith and spirituality.

The crowd's frenzy quickly drowns my thoughts while silencing the pounding hooves, kicking up dirt, as the horses near the finish line.

"Winner!" he exclaims. "What did I tell you?" I do my best to show signs of enthusiasm.

We catch up with Auguste's friend, Georges, who I am told is an art professor at the university.

"Victory!" shouts Georges as we approach.

"You have repeated history." Auguste embraces his friend. "Will the others never learn their lesson?"

"Let us hope not, as they are always needed to fatten the purse." Georges wipes his forehead with a handkerchief and steps to his side to introduce his companion. "And this is my good-luck charm, Cassandra Grigoravich."

"And another one of your pupils?" asks Auguste.

"Indeed," he says. "It is rare to find beauty, artistry, and horse sense confined in one woman."

"I have a knack for finding comfort in the company of sophisticated gentlemen," she says, her eyes looking to me for a response.

"She means old gentlemen," says Georges, laughing.

"That is obvious." Auguste laughs. "And this is Nora Thorsen, a sweet flower plucked from across the ocean."

"My pleasure," I say nervously and with a slight curtsey.

The four of us gather around a table near the concessions. An order for a round of drinks is placed, and Georges inquires as to my tastes in horses.

"I am a lowly farm girl. I have dealt mostly with old draft horses."

"But, surely," he asks, "you can spot a horse with winning form when you see it?"

"I am no expert, afraid to say."

"Have you and Monsieur Valadon been acquainted long?" asks Cassandra.

"We met in New York City only last July."

"I hope you will find Paris equally exciting and rewarding as New York."

I think to say more than "thank you," but words elude me as I look into Cassandra's eyes and see both warmth and confidence.

❧

*June 1900*

The evening air is filled with the warmth of old friends, the sounds of leisure, and the smell of meals in preparation. It has been a productive day for Auguste, as he has finally captured on canvas a certain aspect of light reflection off the Seine, a glint off the waves, that blinds the eye for one moment and creates the illusion of shade the next.

As he and I sit with a number of his friends at the Bistro Le Grand, his friend, Georges, ponders the process. "I don't doubt your efforts, my friend," he pleads, "but I am merely contemplating the evolution of your style."

"Evolution comes with age. Is that not obvious?" Auguste sits with his hands clasped together in his lap and speaks smugly, as though he is addressing the entire universe. "Viva immortality!"

"Careful, Auguste, that you don't knock heads with the spirit of Denis while you bathe yourself in eternity."

There is a chorus of laughter, and I speak to Georges. "Who is this Denis you speak of?"

"Nora," he begins as he takes three successive gulps from his *aperitif*, "there is a very old saint who walks these environs."

"Yes, Georges," Auguste instructs. "You know Nora has much to learn about Paris, so please provide accurate details and none of your usual revisionist illustrations."

I can see Georges's face turning red, not from Auguste's advisory, but rather from the Pastis, which he consumes at a combination of two parts to one part rather than the customary five to one. "But the historical version will only dull the evening's festivities." He lifts his glass in the air, his sweaty pate gleaming from the sunset, jowls trembling, and in spite of his consumptive condition, bellows a proclamation, "Here! Here! It is the patriotic right of all Frenchmen to embellish the history of the nation!"

Cheers are sparse as Georges continues his tale. "But to your point, my dear Nora, the old saint wanders about the city, carrying his head in hand after having it chopped off. It was how he was thanked for coming to convert the local pagans back to Christianity."

Auguste, still pleased with himself, adds, "And you should be careful you don't suffer the same fate at the hands of the Impressionists, Georges." This is followed by uproarious laughter.

My appreciation for both these elderly artists and their love of life has increased immensely over the past six months. There is a sweet timelessness about their lives that hints at a sense of immortality nearly equal to God's. I believe even as they know they are growing old and will die someday, they do not fear death, as they absorb the moments of joy and solitude they find from time to time, both from their art and friendship. It is at these same times I am less bound to my

Christian roots and, instead, relieved by what Tristan had referred to as the absurdity of life.

Our waiter brings us the evening's special of pork chops served with button mushrooms and onions. The aroma clashes with the stench of dead fish that just now appears. No one else seems to notice. At least for the moment, the lively conversation and delicious food are a pleasant diversion from the letter I received from my sister, Ida, first thing this morning. Like all her previous letters, it leaves me conflicted.

> *Dearest Nora,*
>
> *I think it is wonderful news that you are in Paris, and I find myself envious of how brave you are to venture so far from home. I hope you are leading a rich and fulfilling life.*
>
> *Everyone here is doing well. I think Mama really misses you not being here, but maybe that is due to the absence of your laundry skills. Of course, I am only kidding, dear sister.*
>
> *My first school term was a great success, but I am very glad to be home for the summer. I had quite a few smart young students in my class. One such student, Mabel Hendricks, proved herself to be quite apt in learning her subjects. I think you will find this surprising when you recall the obstacles she has encountered her entire childhood.*
>
> *I am not so sure I will be teaching this coming fall, as I have a suitor. He is a fine gentleman from Crookston, and his occupation is that of a land surveyor. He is both handsome and thought-*

*ful. I am quite taken with him and even had the occasion to break one of the rules of my teaching contract by keeping company with him one Saturday afternoon in April when I believed the elderly couple whom I was boarding with would be gone for several hours. This was entirely my fault, as I encouraged it, even while my young gentleman was discouraging it.*

There is never a mention of Ella, only the reassurance of a supportive family from across the Atlantic. And today's letter also included a short letter from my young brother, Teddy. His tenth birthday is in a few weeks, and he wrote accordingly:

*You are missed, sister, by one and all. Peter and I think of you each time we gallop Ezzy through the field where Trygg tumbled from the hay wagon last spring. Remember how hard you laughed?*

*Your brother,*

*Teddy*

*July 1900*
Some overcast days, the view from the basilica of Sacred Heart church in Paris provides nothing but loneliness. I can see Paris for miles, quietly reminding me how far from home I am and how much a foreigner I truly am. Auguste teaches me to paint the best he

can, but he has little patience for my lack of dedication. I explain to him over and over how the mechanics elude me.

"Worry less about the mechanics," he reiterates, "and, instead, feel that which is moving inside you. You have a spirit, do you not?"

"I have a spirit for many things. But perhaps not for painting."

"Paint what you feel, Nora. Don't fall prey to the reality of the scene."

But, alas, another good lesson has gone to waste.

I wander over to where Cassandra is drawing. She is trying to capture the definition of the Montmartre Vineyard for later paintings commissioned by a winery from Savoie.

"They are nearly ripe," I say.

"Yes. They will be quite expressive in my work once we have clear skies. I hope to precede the harvest."

"There is so much culture here, and you seem so acclimated to it all."

"Three years at university has helped me to blend in with the beauty of Paris."

"But don't you ever miss home?"

"I am home enough. I don't miss it. But you, Nora, do you ever plan on returning to your homeland?"

"It is a difficult story to tell." I slowly shake my head.

"But you will tell me someday, yes?"

"Yes." The conversation does little to improve my mood.

"Let me draw you, Nora." She sets down her pad and pencil and takes me by the hand, pulling me up from off the retaining wall. "I think you will look best standing here with the cityscape in the background. I think I can make you look like a real citizen of Paris. Then you can see yourself as one whenever you look at it. Agreed?"

I smile and nod. "Perhaps you wouldn't mind teaching me your native language."

"Ukrainian? But it is such an ugly sounding language when compared to French."

"I don't think so. Your voice makes it sound pleasing to the ear."

Cassandra smiles and shrugs. "If you like."

❦

So much study dulls the senses. A mid-afternoon break is in order. Cassandra drags me by the hand, rushing down the street, our steps clicking off the cobblestone. Then she lets go of me, and our running becomes uneven as I fall behind. I see her looking back at me with a look of concern. I imagine she already knows what troubles me.

We duck into our favorite little café that holds half a dozen stools lining the bar and three small, white, metal tables, each with two iron-wire chairs. We sit at the one closest to the window, our usual table. I imagine the café to be just another room in the apartment Auguste has provided for me, only the walk from one room to the next is very, very far.

The owner looks up from his newspaper without a change in expression. I'm sure we have interrupted his solitude, as there are no other customers. He sets his paper down.

"Tell me, Nora, what is the matter?" Cassandra pulls her chair over next to mine.

"It is Auguste," I begin. "I think I am about to overstay my welcome."

"What do you mean?"

Just then, the owner brings us our regular drinks without a word.

"*Merci.*" I finger the glass and measure my words. "Auguste wishes to do a portrait of me in a compromising position."

"Is that all?" Cassandra is already slouching in her seat.

"Is that *all?*" I repeat.

"It is nothing. My first time, two years ago with Georges, there was nervousness, but I was soon comfortable."

"But there is so much at stake."

"Indeed. If you wish to be an artist, you will find benefit from both sides of the easel."

"Therein is the difference between us. I am not sure that I am intended to be an artist."

"But you traveled all this way with Auguste. I didn't want to believe you to be in love with him, so I imagined you were here to learn to become an artist."

I know it is finally time to share with Cassandra my true reasons for leaving America. In spite of the heaviness of the world outside, the intimacy of the little café makes it easy for the words to flow, to get it all out, and to know that I have found a real friend in whom I can confide.

"You were blessed for all those years, Nora, to have had such a close companion. I truly envy you."

"But surely you have deep, long-held feelings for someone close to you."

"Not me. I am a spoiled child. Or at least I used to be. I think you have helped me become a better person. Even though I am not religious, I appreciate your spirituality. You have a sense about the universe that is both simple and innocent."

"That is naivety, something I have come to realize in myself. Something I wish to replace with experience and understanding."

She smiles. "You may find, over time, it is easier to change ideas than it is to change who you are."

We clink our glasses together without a word but knowing we had sealed our friendship.

My relationship with Cassandra gives me a sense of betrayal. I know I am so much more inhibited with Auguste than I am with her. We have become nearly attached at the hip, which is quite strange. I feel we have little in common, other than we both are intimately attached to older men. I am like a country peasant whose thick Norwegian-American accent stands out like a church organ in a saloon, while she is like a metropolitan trollop, displayed by her unfeminine mannerisms, slouching while seated with one bare ankle up on the table. But somehow we manage to complement one another in Parisian settings. If I have chosen to be a fish out of water, it is nice to have company. And the more I learn to speak and write her native language, the closer our bond.

Cassandra and I enjoyed a ride on the *Grand Roue de Paris*, a giant Ferris wheel built specifically for the Fair. The enclosed passenger cars are large and spacious as we reach the peak, which, I am told, is one hundred meters.

We are now walking back to the Montmartre district. It is nearing dusk, and the wind is blowing from a direction that seems to allow the bells of Notre Dame to ring distinctly. Cassandra and I are holding hands as we walk, but now she stops suddenly to listen to the sound of the bells.

"Do you hear that?" she asks me.

"Of course, I hear it, all the time every day."

"I know, but this time is different."

"Yes. It sounds much clearer than usual. It must be the wind."

"I don't know about that. I just know that there are no people around. It is just you and me sharing the ringing of the bells."

"Do you believe it is a sign?"

"Perhaps."

"Really? A sign of what?"

"A sign of the future," she says, laughing and running down the street with me in tow.

Cassandra drags me to the Moulin Rouge. It is a festive place with much to see, some of which is not fit for the eyes of decent people. The bohemian atmosphere reeks of hedonism and carnality. I can feel something momentous occurring both within the cabaret and within me. It is a feeling I define as beauty, freedom, and truth. I am all at once caught up in the artistry of the moment. I don't know whether to blame it on the spirits of liquor or my desire to escape the pretentious life I have been living up to this point.

An operetta is in motion when we arrive, and crowd participation offstage is not discouraged. I follow Cassandra around like an over-excited poodle. I think I am at the end of my rope when she pulls me into a crowd that is more boisterous than the entire crowd itself. The two of us partake in a saucy rendition of some archaic French number. We are both beyond exhaustion at the conclusion. Then Cassandra is gone, pulled from my grip, and I am left standing in the midst of chaos. I search for her, but there are so many people, arms, and legs flailing about. I spy a higher setting, where people are elevated, seated or standing in a sort of side stage. I make my way through the crowd, and after a great effort, I am able to look across the ballroom over the heads of the crowd. But even this position does not provide a good view. I am about to give up when I hear laughter behind me. There are two people on the floor in the corner. I instantly recognize Cassandra's dress, which has been compromised by the hands of a stranger.

"And this, Pierre, is my good friend Nora," Cassandra shouts.

I go to lift her from the floor. The man begins to laugh and frees Cassandra from his embrace.

"We are off, Pierre," says Cassandra feigning a pouty disposition.

"Don't forget the address, Cassandra," says Pierre, who makes no effort to get up from the floor and, instead, gives us a half-hearted wave and appears to ball up in the corner so as to take a nap.

I pull Cassandra by her wrist through the garden and to the exit, passing the giant wooden elephant along the way.

"Do you know what goes on inside the big elephant, Nora?"

"Yes, Cassandra, you already told me."

"A very sweet belly dancer. But she is for the amusement of men only."

"I know, Cassandra, I know." She is heavy, and I am tired. "Can you help me walk, Cassandra?"

But instead of helping me, she stops in her tracks, resting her arms on my shoulders, and begins to lament. "Do you know what is my only life's regret, Nora?"

"No, Cassandra, I don't know."

"Falling for a belly dancer."

"That's very sad, Cassandra. I'm sorry for your one regret in life." I am joking, as I could think of a number of instances where she had expressed regret. Not being a well-mannered child. Not taking her studies seriously. Not accepting the marriage proposal from one of the most influential businessmen in all of Kiev.

"Don't be. It is a good regret. She was a good model. She gave me all the best poses for my nudes when I was going through my Victorian phase."

"That is wonderful, Cassandra. Now let me take you home."

"You know what is so comical about the art of belly dancing?"

I shake my head imperceptibly.

"All those women from that period were offended by the belly dancer, but they too had the bellies of a belly dancer. They were too restricted by their moral code to realize they could have made good belly dancers. It is funny, is it not?"

"It is funny. Let me take you home now."

But before I can redirect her to the exit, she bends down and claws at my stomach. "This is not the belly of a belly dancer," she proclaims. "It is too rigid, too firm. This is the belly of a milk maiden."

I lift her up, and we are once again walking toward the exit.

"Take me home, Nora." I can just barely hear her above the din of the crowd. "And remember, my heart breaks very easily."

<hr/>

Auguste is a gifted artist. I'm no expert, but I believe he is capturing the essence of the new style practiced by the less-respected artists who reside in the Montmartre section of the city. I suspect his involvement in this latest movement can only elevate their stature over time. I love many of his landscapes. The light, colors, and depth move me. I am a farm girl, so all I know of landscapes are grand stretches of wheat and barley fields. Golden, blue, and symmetrical they may be, but by contrast, Auguste's landscapes flow, providing contour I have never seen before.

"Allow me to vent," he would say, pounding fist to palm, amongst his peers. "If Louis the Fourteenth were alive today, he should have his head lopped off for the destruction he caused much of the city's gardens." Of course, no one dared disagree, as all understood his passion for art. "And then to rely on English interpretation?" he would continue. "Preposterous!"

Today is not about landscape but rather about the portrait he proposes to make of me. He asks very politely, in fact, very lovingly. Again, my need for debt repayment begins to emerge. "There is a summer day awaiting our presence. Let us not squander it indoors but rather partake of the earthly joys of wine, song, and passion."

"How would you pose me?" I already know the answer and make an attempt to avoid the topic. After all, his studio is filled with very provocative nudes. Many of his subjects are less prudish than others. "What will you do with this one?" I ask about a sizeable canvas whose chestnut-haired, pale-skinned subject lay prone, appearing to invite a seducer out of view. Her small breasts do not compliment her wide hips. Her left hand hovers above her partially open mouth, the back of the forefinger brushing against both her upper and lower lips the color of coquettish rouge. Somehow, I find it both mesmerizing and repulsive.

"This is not a candidate for the Louvre," Auguste explains, matter-of-fact in tone. "This is for my personal whimsy."

"As far as posing," he continues, "I would like to paint you *au natural,* with hair flowing around your shoulders."

Of course I understand what he is suggesting, but I find this incomprehensible. He has already done several portraits with me fully clothed, all of which I find flattering. To be alone, half nude at the very least, in

Auguste's studio does not appeal to me. It's not that I do not trust him, but rather, I feel this is too compromising to my being, to who I am as a person. Is not my shame overwhelming enough?

"I have a spot down river, very secluded, with good light an hour on both sides of the high sun." He runs his fingers through his long, graying hair while twirling his watch chain back and forth around his forefinger. His brown eyes are focusing so hard, I cannot help but blush. "You have a natural beauty that I must capture at once."

"When?" I ask, resignedly.

"Now? It is okay then?"

It must be, I tell myself, as I nod.

❦

We arrive with time enough for Auguste to set up his easel and to pose me in the best possible light. The commotion he creates by banging tripod and clattering bottles of finely mixed paints does nothing to help ease my discomfort.

"What a surprise," pronounces Auguste.

"What is?"

"Your golden hair. It reminds me of my sister's when she was a little girl."

I feel like a little girl lost in the vastness of the world around me. "Where is she now?"

"Alas, she is gone to the heavens."

"I'm so sorry."

"Merci." He dabs brush to paint, striking the palette with vigor, like a woodpecker with a muffled beak. "Will you disrobe, ma cherie?"

I undo my blouse slowly, haphazardly. Auguste senses my apprehension immediately.

"Nora," he begins, "we have been together these past six months, and haven't I been the perfect gentleman?"

"Yes," I say, "the perfect gentleman."

"What else can I do to assure you my intentions are pure?"

I shrug and then ask, "Maybe if I had a better understanding of art?"

"That is a very good observation." He puzzles over this concept and begins by explaining the essence of art, particularly the portrait. "If I may, I think the most basic fundamental of art is that you understand that the spirit and nature are in harmony."

This is a new concept for me, and I begin to give it much consideration. But just then, I hear rustling in the nearby woods and quickly cover my shoulders.

We both pause to listen.

I begin buttoning my blouse. "I'm so very sorry, Auguste."

"It is of little consequence." He chuckles half-heartedly. "Perhaps another day when the woods are less mysterious."

In the end, I fear I have broken Auguste's heart.

There is little about Cassandra that reminds me of Ella. Her face is much narrower with high, strong cheekbones. And her eyes appear always to be sad, even when she smiles. She manages a wave in her auburn hair that is at once askew and nicely placed over her right ear.

Cassandra, at times, loses me with her thick Ukrainian accent, as well as with her sonorous French dialect and broken English. She is three years my senior and so much more worldly than I. She challenges my faith while I grow fond of her each passing day.

I am filled with joy each time Cassandra visits me in my little apartment. A visitor makes me feel less of a kept woman. She is the ears my saddened voice craves during these dark times.

Today she helps me bathe, caressing my neck and shoulders with the soft touch of an artist's hand. The melodic reciting of a Baudelaire poem, which I find to be both decadent and arousing, fills the room.

> *The strong beauty kneeling before the frail*
> *beauty,*
> *Superb, she savored voluptuously*
> *The wine of her triumph and stretched out*
> *toward the girl*
> *As if to reap her reward of sweet thankfulness.*

The quietness of the room and the afternoon breeze through the window make me weep while reflecting on similar occasions shared with Ella. But rather than poetry, she would recite verse, mostly from the book of Psalm.

"Do you know how lonely I have become since running from America?"

"It is obvious. Your eyes bear this out."

"And my eyes see so much of my past in your eyes." I say this like a drunkard, suggesting both innuendo and confusion.

"When you come to that place where you know inner peace, it will be because you have let go of the past. And far be it for me to keep you there. I fear our friendship is not a good one."

"That's quite funny, Cassandra," I say, looking up to her with smiling eyes. "I speak of loneliness, and you speak of deserting me?"

"Don't mind me, Nora," she says, assuring while kneading the back of my shoulders. "We Ukrainians have a way of mixing our emotions so that they create confusion. Forget what I say."

"Forgetting is the hard part." I take her hands in mine and lean back in the tub.

"*Ti krasivaya*," she whispers.

"*Ti milaya*," I say, pressing her hands to my cheek.

✦

My encounters with Auguste, less frequent now, are filled with guilt. Although I feel I have taken advantage of his good nature and charity while not repaying him with what I suspect he truly desires, he is always happy to see me.

Today we meet for lunch at the Café DeMour, near the docks where the start of the weekly yacht races takes place.

"Yes, there is something noticeably different about you." He smiles, leaning back in his chair and rolling the top of his cane between his hands with the precision of an artist.

It is so difficult to meet with Auguste knowing I will rendezvous with Cassandra shortly. I compound my shame with each passing moment by partaking of his generosity.

"Won't you stay a little longer, Nora? I hardly see you these days."

I now wish only to tell Auguste why this is. But I forget how he looks young for his age and quite wise in years.

"I think I know what is going on." He is smiling. "Nora has taken my advice. She has found love in Paris, no?"

I search quickly for the answer but feel only doubt. I shake my head and laugh. "You are mistaken, Auguste. I'm far, far from the hopeless romantic you are."

⁂

I am seated outside the little apartment when Cassandra approaches. I smarten my demeanor and hope she does not sense my glumness.

"Nora, I have come to save you from yourself." She drops down next to me, rolling her shoulder into mine. "I have secured for us passage to my homeland. I have found for you a place farther east for you to rekindle your faith."

Cassandra's excitement pulls me out of my despair. *Faith* is a word that has been missing from my vocabulary for a long time.

"Are you familiar with the Russian novelist Tolstoy?" she asks.

"Of course. I read his novel *Anna Karenina* two summers ago. I thought the story quite moving."

"Yes, but now—"

"Though, unlike most readers, I did not find much sympathy for Anna."

"Whether you keep that to yourself or share with the count is entirely up to you."

"The count?"

"Listen to what I am trying to tell you."

I brace myself for Cassandra to tell me more about Tolstoy.

"My family has ties to the count by way of a mutual friend. I have been in contact with him to secure you employment on the count's estate."

"But what would I do?"

"I say you could teach."

"Teach what? I am not a teacher."

"I told them you are American and could teach English. And there was mention of translating works to English and French."

"My French is much improved. But you know my Russian is non-existent."

"Russian is nearly cousin to Ukrainian, which you are learning at an accelerated speed."

"You must tell me more about this place. It sounds so formal, so aristocratic."

"That is the strangeness of it all."

"How do you mean?"

"The count is a count in title only. He has cast aside all worldliness and has taken to a life of servitude to God."

Though I find this piece of information intriguing, I am now apprehensive about sharing in Cassandra's enthusiasm. I am afraid of becoming an instrument, once again, for yet another aristocrat. My knowledge of Tolstoy is limited. I need to learn more.

"I can see you are overwhelmed by my news."

"But I am most appreciative of what you are doing. I know I have become quite the bore over the past several weeks, and I think you understand why."

"I do, and that is why I have come to save you."

She reaches into her bag, pulls out a book, and hands it to me.

"I think this will help you decide on what you should do."

I take from her a little book with a title that reads *A Confession*.

Such enlightenment! I have spent—no, wasted the past months delving into the sophistries of the philosophical sciences, allowing my sense of right and wrong to be altered and misguided by their gray explanations. When all at once, the answer I seek is given to me out of the kind sacrifice from my new friend.

I have spent the past several days reading the booklet given to me by Cassandra, as well as other writings by Tolstoy. Even so, I cannot lift myself high enough off the ground to feel God's grace. So today I pay the tour fee and elevate with several people to the top of the Eiffel Tower. The wind blows hard, like a storm wishing to either displace me from this pinnacle or chastise me for not coming to my senses. I grow abstract in my thoughts, blocking out those around me, and embrace the warmth of God's breath as he whispers in my ear to make amends, to find the path least traveled by true sinners such as me.

I feel I have been prideful since leaving home. And the little book given to me by Cassandra only accentuates that feeling. I believe I now know what I must do with my life. It is not too late for me to live godly, to wrest my soul from temptation and to engage in endeavors worthy of God's praise. That I am still young enough to realize this causes me much joy. By contrast, Tolstoy was middle aged before confessing he had wasted so many years attaining fame and fortune rather than serving God and mankind.

I look far off to the west, to home, and begin my confession. *I was wrong to hold Ella to a promise she could not keep.* My confession does little to comfort me. If it is intended to clear my conscience, I dismiss such a notion immediately. I turn to look over my shoulder from the shout of a little boy. *I agree to go quietly but not on terms either specious or pious.* After all, tribute, penance, and self-rebuke are simple tools when faced with a grave sin. *I will make amends by living according to God's plan for as long as he graces me with the breath of life. Why? Because it is the right thing… the only fair thing to do for what I have done to Ella.*

I find Auguste working frantically in his studio. I hesitate to disturb him, but what I must tell him cannot wait, as Cassandra and I leave by train first thing in the morning.

"I shouldn't wish to bother you, Auguste, as you appear to be involved in a very important painting."

"It's a commissioned work I promised to have finished several days ago. Don't know why. Just look at it. Between you and me, Nora, the woman has no life in her, no spirituality, and the portrait suffers as a result. Will I never learn?"

"I'm afraid to tell you that I'm going away from here."

Auguste stops looking at the portrait. He stares down at the floor, and his arms go limp. The brush in his hand that was alive with energy just moments ago now appears to be but an extra elongated finger. "When do you leave?"

"Tomorrow morning."

"It's Cassandra, isn't it?"

"It's not about Cassandra. Well, perhaps a little."

"She has bewitched you, just as you bewitched me several months ago."

"Please don't be angry, Auguste. I feel I am not cut out to be an artist's mistress, let alone an artist. I don't know who I am, but I know I have strayed from my true path."

"How can I be angry?" He speaks as if overcome by a wave of relief. "You have given me great joy these past many months."

"And I have enjoyed your hospitality and company. Unfortunately, I have not found what I am looking for in your gay city." I explain my resolve to travel to Russia and why.

"And so you should go. You need to find the proper remedy to heal your soul."

I look up in his eyes, searching for the meaning in their twinkle as well as the words expressed by such a kind, wise Frenchman. I can't help myself from smiling. He takes me by my shoulders and pulls me to him.

"Don't stop sketching and painting, Nora. Someday you will find a place where you will feel the passion that creates beautiful paintings. Trust me."

Auguste's eyes glisten. I think how much I love his passion for art and how saddened I am by his love for me. I feel shame for misjudging his true intentions all these months. If I were wise, I would have known all along that he truly is the purest of artists.

"Will you ever return to America, Nora?"

"I have so much to answer for. As such, it would be difficult to face those who I have wronged. But maybe someday. Why do you ask?"

"Just curious. I have a gift for you, but I think it best to send it ahead of you for the day you return to your homeland."

"Oh, that seems cruel, Auguste. Shouldn't you give it to me here and now?"

"I think where you are going will help you, in time, to appreciate many things about your past."

At the moment, I feel Auguste's true gift to be that of remaining my friend though I leave him so abruptly.

❧

*September 1900*

"I recognize this word," I tell Cassandra, pointing to the newspaper where the headline reads *Assassino Trovato Colpevole*. Would you mind translating the story for me?"

"Of course, I will try. But my Italian is not so good."

I watch her focus intently as our train makes its way from Milan to Venice. We have spent a day shopping the markets in the city square of Milan. I feel Cassandra was trying to tempt me with her expensive tastes, but I am not to be deterred. I am due in Yasnaya Polyana in a week's time and am determined to make schedule.

"Ah, now I understand," she begins, her tone quite flippant. "This is the trial of the assassin who killed the king of Italy this past summer. He was found guilty."

"Killing a king? Does it say why?"

"I remember discussing this with Georges and some others. There was much discussion about what nerve one must possess in order to kill a king."

"A mad man, I would think." The late August sun shines brightly against the countryside. I am content to listen to Cassandra's voice as the train moves slowly up a steep grade.

"This is not a mad man. This man, Bresci, is a simple man who is determined to rid his country of this king after the king killed innocent people protesting high bread prices."

"That does not sound like a king to me but rather a tyrant."

"So then, my dear Nora, who do you believe to be worse between tyrant and anarchist?"

I have never thought of it in that way. "It's so political; I can't say without considering all the facts."

"Where you're headed, you'll see that politics and religion are finely mixed together, so much so you may not know one from the other. Russia is ripe for anarchy after so many centuries of tyrants."

"Look, Cassandra, the mountains!"

"Yes, those are the Three Peaks of Veneto. Watch them grow as we get closer and closer to Venice."

From the plains of the Midwest United States to the mountains of Europe, I have come to learn not all things are black and white. There are reasons why tyrants and anarchists behave as they do. And there are reasons why simple people, like me, behave as we do.

I want to find a cause to believe in. I want to be swept up in something worthy of God's blessings.

❧

The sky is a warm blue as our train passes through the turquoise-colored Laguna just before entering Venice. The air is humid, filled with the Mediterranean Sea warmly blowing in from the south. The depot is loud with the sounds of anxious travelers meshing paths of coming and going.

Cassandra decides our every move, as she is familiar with the city, which allows me to take in the ancient sites. We are to reach our hotel by boat, which I find both peculiar and enchanting, as the streets are filled with water. There are no shorelines, but only strong, manmade embankments. I think how different it feels to float down a city street made of water as compared to the quiet, muddy river that runs through the deep woods back home.

I ask Cassandra the names of the great sculptures we pass. Some are just above street level while others are set high upon the roofs of centuries-old buildings. She names every one, as she is a pure student of art.

We leave our things with the front desk of the hotel and begin a tour of the city.

"I don't have an appreciation for these works," she tells me. "I am a painter."

"But how can you not?" I ask, astonished by her indifference and enthralled by my own excitement. "They are so much more alive than paintings."

"To me, Nora, they are lifeless and cold."

"Cassandra, can you not imagine how there are no paintings in the world as old as these statues?"

"Oh, Nora, you are so fixated on immortality."

I end up admitting to myself that Cassandra is right about the power of paintings. We spend not nearly enough time in the Church of Saint Roch. I cannot absorb enough of the works of Jacopo Tintoretto. I am sure these are what I would aspire to paint if I could do a fine enough job of it. The message conveyed by each one of Christ's last days penetrates my very soul.

From there, we spend all afternoon wandering the city and enjoying all the sights and sounds. When we finally begin the journey back to the hotel, the bell towers begin a symphony of ringing.

"It must be six o'clock," says Cassandra.

"How do you know?"

"Every day, the city sings promptly at six."

We climb the stone stairs to our third-floor room. Our accommodations are both quaint and comfortable.

There is a small balcony with just enough room for two people to step out onto. I can see, over the red-tile rooftops, the sun beginning to settle on the horizon just beyond the Laguna.

"Come, Nora. We will go to the square for a bite."

We walk out to the back of the hotel onto a marble terrace, where there are empty tables and chairs, and just below it is a small waterway. I follow Cassandra over a little arched walkway bridging the back entrance to the hotel and a sidewalk leading past other hotels and apartments.

The hum of the crowd just beneath the sporadic sounds of music grows as we approach the Plaza. There are pigeons flying above the crowds in grand disorder. Many find the nearby rooftops while others land on the Plaza concrete, where there are no tables or crowds, only to take flight once again.

We take our seats at a little table deep inside the crowd. Cassandra places our order while we each enjoy a cup of delicious local coffee. I find myself reinvigorated after our long train ride. But something else has infected my good mood. I feel a sense of fraternity among all the joyful people surrounding us. There is a contagion in the air, something filled with both excitement and passion.

We spend the evening on the square, and later, after the sun has disappeared, there is a steady stream of fireworks. The sky is alive with color and noise, but the people around me are even more so, as everyone is engaged in boisterous laughter and flirtatious merriment.

We start our walk back to the hotel, and I notice a line of gondolas docked near the square. I take Cassandra by the wrist. "You will think me quite childish, but I would very much like to ride in a gondola."

"Perhaps one last indulgence," she jests, bowing and waving me to step aboard, "before you lose yourself in the servitude of humanity?"

"Perhaps." I curtsy while looking at the friendly face of the gondolier.

Cassandra and I look up to the stars as we lean back in the front of the gondola. Our driver provides smooth, even strokes through the watery streets. We hold hands as he steers through a narrow, dark passageway lined with buildings that feels like a comfortable blanket.

I imagine for a moment that our driver is not there as Cassandra squeezes my hand tightly. I look at her and smile just as the gondola begins to vibrate.

Our driver stops stroking the water. I hold my breath and squeeze Cassandra's hand in return. "What is it?" I ask.

"Earthquake," she whispers.

The earth rumbles. The once serene water beneath us begins to slosh from side to side, creating small waves against the reflecting darkness while causing the gondola to bob up and down. I look to see lights flickering up and down the waterway, and I begin hearing bells ringing from various corners of the city. At first they are soft and distant but then grow loud and clumsy, underlined by the clatter of nearby chimes. And just as quickly as it starts, the quaking stops.

"Are you frightened, Nora?"

"A little." The sound of bells begins to fade.

"It is your first time, isn't it?"

"Yes." I am trembling, and the air feels suddenly cool.

"Not mine. I have felt the earth move many, many times."

Cassandra wraps her arms around me and nuzzles her nose in the curve of my neck. I want to kiss her forehead, but the earthquake rattles my memories of the day's sights. I have seen a number of perspectives of the crucifixion of Christ, all of which are a reminder that I have committed myself to a life of redemption. I will make it a constant reminder henceforth.

"So much excitement, Cassandra, and now I am so tired."

***

Kiev appears as old as Paris. The streets are soaked when Cassandra and I arrive this morning, but the sunshine provides a combination of warmth and coolness.

"Nora, I see we are early; my carriage has yet to arrive. Let's take tea just down the street at Lipsky Mansion, a fine restaurant, indeed. You can wait there with me until your train continues on its way."

"It is a very fine restaurant," I say with a suspicious eye on Cassandra. The elegance of the interior is softened by the dark mahogany paneling. "I think we should say our farewells now."

"Whatever do you mean?" I have long since grown accustomed to her coyness.

"Let me tell you something, Cassandra." I take her hand in mine, pulling her outside the entrance of the restaurant. "There is a part of me that wishes I could fall in love in a city like Venice or could want to live a life as luxurious as the one you lead. But there is another part of me that seeks God's forgiveness."

"I know, Nora. There is no need for explanation. I am a silly woman who imagines things she ought not to." She kisses my hand. "Promise me we will always be friends."

I gather her in my arms. "The best of friends," I promise while kissing her on the lips.

Cassandra holds me tight as the train engine idles back up the street, hissing steam, and then she whispers in my ear, "I will never see you again, will I?"

"Nonsense," I retort, fighting back tears. "You will come to visit someday, won't you?"

"My family is rich like the Tolstoys, but they choose to live as rich people, not as paupers. That is a change that will not come easy."

I walk quickly back to the passenger car. My vision is blurred, and my nose begins to run. As I board the train, I turn at the top of the steps to wave to Cassandra, but she has vanished.

# *For I Know the Plans
I Have For You*

"For I know the plans I have for you," declares
the Lord, "plans to prosper and not to harm
you, plans to give you hope and a future."

Jeremiah 29:11

❧

The sun is high and the air humid as I arrive at the
Tula station.

"Are you the American?"

I turn to see a bearded man, the owner of the gruff
voice, dressed in a drab gray outfit that appears to be
an old uniform with the patches removed. The beard
hides the expression of disapproval that seems to ema-
nate from his words.

"I am." I stand still, uncertain as to whether I should
move on. Cassandra had put me on notice how com-
monplace it is for the tsar's secret police, the Okhrana,
to harass the Tolstoyans.

"And are these your luxuries?" He points to my
travel chest.

"Yes, but I assure you it contains no contraband."

He appears puzzled. "I ... I am Andre Dimitrovich,
here to collect you and to bring you to Yasnaya
Polyana."

My escort grabs me by my arm and waist and lifts me onto the buckboard, and then he tosses my travel chest into the back of the wagon.

"Thank you for meeting me."

"I have fallen behind in the day's chores." He jolts the reins, and we begin to move down the street, the strong smell of coal filling my nostrils as we pass by several factories with stacks billowing black smoke.

I can see government-style buildings up a number of streets as we enter urban neighborhoods. Before too long, we are riding through quiet countryside, where thatched-roof homes begin to pop up.

My escort's disinterest in me and intimation that my arrival is nothing more than an inconvenience makes it easy to avoid small talk.

In a heavily wooded curve along the road, we come upon three men on horseback. They are dressed in uniforms, but I still fret that they might be road bandits.

I believe Andre senses my concern and instructs me as though I am a child. "Don't speak."

The three horsemen make an effort to stand in front of us, using their mounts as a barricade. The one in the middle shouts, "Halt!" His voice is more threatening than his round head, which appears as waxy as a jack o' lantern.

Andre pulls back on the reins. He leans forward, appearing not at all stressed by the encounter.

"Are you Andre Dimitrovich of Yasnaya Polyana?"

"I am." Without as much as a glance, he hands me the reins and makes motion to stand.

"By order of the provincial government, we are required to stop and question you and search your wagon."

"It is common," he tells me as he jumps down from the wagon.

"You two," the one in charge instructs the others, "search the wagon while I question Andre Dimitrovich." He waves Andre over.

I think to continue staring forward rather than making eye contact, but I am unable to resist looking at the two men rummaging through the back of the wagon. I find their efforts both mechanical and arbitrary, as though they have done this on one too many occasions. Imagining that it will help our predicament, I offer them each a cigarette from the remaining box Cassandra had given me. They willingly accept.

While they fiddle with lighting them, I notice Andre appears to be quite animated with his interrogator. I then notice Andre looking in my direction before handing what appears to be a piece of paper to the man. They both walk back to the wagon.

A soft breeze whispers through the trees as the three men mount and ride off. Andre motions for the team to start again down the road.

Just as I am about to ask Andre about his conversation with the interrogator, he says, "You should not have given them your cigarettes. It does no good."

"But I have no use for them, as there is no smoking permitted where we're going, correct?"

"It does not look good on the community should word get around that we are going against our own tenets."

I take his point to heart, now realizing it was not a very smart thing to have done. "I guess I wasn't thinking. I thought it would help us in some way."

"It is common for the local police to harass the peasants from Yasnaya Polyana. You should understand it will happen again, and the best thing for you to do is to not interact with them."

We arrive at the stables of Yasnaya Polyana, a short distance from the count's home, accompanied by a warm southerly breeze that brings to life the tops of the tall pine and birch trees lining the gravel road. This is a good feeling, one of home. The country is clean and peaceful with a presence of God.

The local peasant farmers are busy in the fields. The smell of fresh-cut hay brings more memories of my homeland.

"You will help in the fields." Andre's tone is smug. "Maybe you won't smile so much when you are working hard."

"I'm sorry. Does my smiling bother you?"

"Don't be ridiculous. Of course your smiling does not offend me." Now he halts the horses in front of the stable. "I just want you to be aware there is plenty of work for everyone, plenty of good deeds to be performed in the name of Tolstoy."

"That's funny," I say, "I thought all the good deeds were done in the name of God."

"Very well," he mumbles as he jumps down and begins to unhitch the team.

"If it's no trouble, could you tell me where I might find a man called Kenworthy?"

"He works with the count."

"I'm aware of that. But do you know where he might be found?"

"My instructions were only to bring you here." He motions to help me down.

I wave away his efforts and jump down from the wagon. "Never mind. I'll look for him myself."

A breeze is blowing through the trees just beyond the orchard to the west, carrying with it the sweet smell of apples. Cassandra had mentioned the variety of apples growing over the nearly four thousand acres making up the estate.

"Here is Maria Fyodorovna. She will help you to settle into your living quarters."

"You are the American?" The elderly woman greets me with a large smile that matches her large gray-blue eyes.

"Yes. My name is Nora."

"Welcome to Yasnaya Polyana." She takes my hand in hers and squeezes tight, like a familiar aunt. "Come with me, and I will show you where you will be staying."

As we walk along the road, I spot the roof of the count's home just over a little hill looking east. It is quite grand, as I imagined for someone of such greatness.

"Is it a beautiful home inside, Maria Fyodorovna?"

"I have been in it a few times, and yes, it is very lovely inside. The rooms are filled with furniture befitting a king. And the china is rimmed with gold."

"But he is no king, I've been assured."

"Oh, no, my dear, quite the opposite. He is more a peasant than this peasant coming toward us."

I see an elderly man leading a horse and cart emerge from the same cavernous road I arrived on. "Why do you refer to the count as a peasant?"

"He goes about the estate dressed like this one," she says, pointing to the elderly man. "Sometimes he even helps in the fields."

I think to myself how refreshing to hear that someone with so much wealth and privilege is willing to humble himself.

"Old man! Have you finished your deliveries so soon?"

"Am I not here?" His voice sounds soft and filled with wisdom.

"Then you can bring our new American friend to the community."

"I am Misha Popovich, from the village of Barun in the Saratov Oblast." He bows while removing his cap.

"Where might that be?"

"It is northeast of here." He points far off in the distance with an imprecise wave. "You can't miss it. If you fall into the Volga, then you have walked halfway across the Saratov, where the river cuts it in two."

"We have a great river in the state where I come from. In fact, the mouth of this river, called the Mississippi, begins not so far from my home."

"It is a great river?"

"Oh, yes.

"And where does this river end?"

"It is very far from my home."

"I see. The Volga is nearing its end from my home, where it finally empties into the Caspian Sea."

"Enough chatter about rivers. Don't you wish to see where you will be living?"

"Of course, I am ready. But first I must meet with an American named Kenworthy."

"Then I must escort you to the count's house." Misha takes me by the arm, his gentle touch reminding me of Auguste's.

"Be careful of old men from the Saratov Oblast!" Maria continues on her way in the opposite direction.

I smile at Misha.

He pats the back of my hand with his rough palm. "How did you arrive in Yasnaya Polyana?"

"A man named Andre brought me here from the station."

"It is strange that he did not take you to the house to meet the count's assistant."

"No less strange than our encounter on the way here."

"What do you mean?"

"While on the road, we were detained by the local police."

"Are you sure? How were they dressed?"

"Somewhat official looking would be my description."

"They were most likely members of the tsar's secret police. They did not give you much trouble, I trust."

"No. In fact, they appeared to be quite indifferent about their work."

"And your guide? How was he able to circumvent these men?"

"Andre? He was most accommodating." I recall the transaction I witnessed between he and the leader of the group but decide to keep it to myself. I do not wish to appear gossipy. And, besides, I am not interested in getting caught up in the local politics.

We walk to the front door of the estate. I now realize the columns are not so grand and the exterior could use a whitewash.

"Go ahead and knock on the door, child. I will leave you to your business, but rest assured, I will be waiting for you when you are finished. Then I shall take you to your living quarters."

Prior to arriving, I learned I will be helping an assistant to the count, an American named John Kenworthy, translate certain papers. This is to be part-time work. Aside from that, I am expected to help with the communal chores: milking the cows, working the vegetable garden, and helping in the fields. It all sounded promising, and I felt great pride in knowing that my upbringing would help me to adapt to my new environment. And my nurse's training should be well received when needed.

This is the kind of life in which I believe I can best serve God.

A servant answers the door and bids me to be seated in a nearby anteroom. I am there only a few moments when I hear voices and footsteps down the hallway.

"Good day, deputy." The voice sounds rushed as I hear the front door shut. I stand at the sound of approaching steps.

"Miss Thorsen, is it?"

"How do you do?"

"My name is Kenworthy." His demeanor is cordial yet distracted. "You had safe conduct, I trust?"

"Yes, of course."

"Good." I can tell he is miles away. His graying hair is swept back, leaving his forehead bare to reveal three distinct age lines running horizontally and equally parted, like the bars on a sheet of music. "I don't mean to sound dismissive, but I must speak to the count at once, so I must cut our introductory meeting short. I hope you don't mind."

"Not at all." I am ready to depart but can't help but think that I have gotten off on the wrong foot somehow. "Is there something the matter?"

"No concern of yours," he says stiffly, but then he reconsiders his answer, furrowing his brow. "You'll contend soon enough with issues the rest of the community has dealt with as it relates to our tsar. The count is hardly a favorite in Saint Petersburg, if you can imagine."

"I don't understand."

"The count's theories and beliefs run counter to those of the Church and the State. He wields great power over the nation's peasantry. And no tsar wants to play second to another when it comes to the loyalty of the people."

"I should like to learn more, if you think it will help with my work."

"And you shall. That is why you are here. My publishing house wishes very much to translate the count's writings into English. I will need you to assist me in translating them."

"I assure you, I am here to do whatever I can to help the community prosper according to God's plan."

"You have been sent here with a very good reference. I am quite certain you can be trusted."

"But of course."

"The count believes he can no longer rely on the countess to assist him in editing his work. That is why I have taken over that responsibility. But editing is only part of the effort. It also needs to be translated into several languages."

"Excuse me, but I think I should inform you that my grasp of the written Russian language is rudimentary at best."

"No cause for concern, as I shall be the one translating from Russian into Ukrainian. The two are closely related, so I suspect your proficiency in Russian will only improve over time. I need you to translate from Ukrainian to both English and French."

"I see."

"You are, I trust, comfortable with standard Ukrainian?"

"Yes. I had a wonderful instructor the past several months, in both Ukrainian and French."

He nods his approval. "Once translated, the works are to be distributed across borders, as there are no publishing houses in all of Russia that are permitted to print any of the count's latest material."

Just as I find relief from the uncertainty of translating, my mind is just as quickly filled with concern. I now understand that I am falling right into the heart of an effort that could be viewed as anarchistic. I find myself wondering if I could be a part of such an effort.

I recall the count's book *The Kingdom of God Is Within You* as being very critical of both the current Russian government and the Russian Orthodox Church, but I hadn't considered playing an active role in the potential overthrow of the government.

"You still appear troubled." His impatience shows as he teeters from one foot to the other. "May I ask why?"

"Mr. Kenworthy, I don't wish to appear ungrateful for this wonderful opportunity, but I believe I may not be up to the task."

"On what grounds?"

"I think I may be too tentative when it comes to such cloak-and-dagger efforts."

"This is hardly cloak and dagger, my dear lady. This is the evolution of a new way of life. We can hardly be expected to manage a community in direct contradiction to the existing state of the rest of the nation without the threat of intimidation from the government. Nor, I should add, with the duplicity of the church."

"I mean no disrespect, Mr. Kenworthy. It's just my upbringing has taught me to respect the power of the government, whether it is that of Russia or my own country. However, I have come to realize that governments do not always have their people's best interests in mind. And at times, the laws of man are not in unison with those of God."

"I can appreciate your hesitancy in this matter, but I assure you, I will not place you in a compromising position, one that goes against your faith in God or your trust in authority."

I remain apprehensive but smile as Mr. Kenworthy bids me good day and requests that I arrive at nine o'clock the following morning to begin work.

As promised, I find Misha waiting for me on the front steps of the count's home. "All is well between you and the other American?"

"Yes. I found him agreeable."

"Very good. Now we will walk to the village where you will stay."

"Is it far?"

"Only a mile or so."

"Too bad Andre unhitched the wagon."

"We don't burden the animals. Whatever we can do for ourselves on the estate grounds, we do."

"But what about my things?"

"Andre has already carried them down to the village."

Surprised, I conclude that what Andre lacks in manners, he partially makes up in helpfulness.

I conclude my first day of work with Mr. Kenworthy and return to the Friendship Hall for supper just as it is served. The building is very rustic in appearance, both inside and out, but I can smell its newness by the fragrance of birch wood and sap.

"You're just in time," says Katya, a shy, plump woman who befriended me this morning.

A variety of vegetable dishes and several loaves of freshly baked bread are set on the long table that accommodates as many as twenty people. Just like this morning, the women sit on one side, while the men are on the other. And also like this morning, Andre sits directly across from me.

"Nice of you to join us, Nora Nelsovna." His smirking does nothing to improve my opinion of him. "Now that the hard part of preparing the meal has been taken care of." Misha had obviously circulated my father's first name, and now Andre was addressing me with the Russian patronymic, for which I find his tone condescending.

Just as I am about to rebut his accusation that I deliberately avoided kitchen duty, Maria speaks. "I think we would all like to hear of your travels, Nora. Perhaps later this evening, you will share your experiences?"

"I'm afraid, Maria, there is very little to tell. I have only been away from home a short time."

"But we have heard you have come from the great cities of the West," said Misha. "New York. Paris."

"These are very interesting places," I explain, "but there is much evil and sadness to be found. As such, that is why I am here now."

"How do you mean?" asks Maria.

"I am looking to rid myself of the past. I wish to make a fresh start in a new land amongst you fine people."

"I wonder what it is she hides from." Andre addresses everyone as though I am absent.

Misha raps his spoon against the tabletop. "Your curiousness makes me wonder if you're who *you* appear to be," he says while staring at Andre, who appears almost startled. Then he points his spoon at me and explains. "At meal time, we are usually graced with the quiet tongue of Andre Dimitrovich."

"I sense something in the air." Maria smiles, her eyes eager to share something I suspect my ears won't like hearing.

Andre's cheeks just above his beard begin to turn crimson. "This kind of talk does not inspire an appetite." He rises to leave.

Katya leans into me and provides her interpretation. "I think he likes you."

I smile at her round, curious face and whisper, "I'm afraid I'm not very good at romance, Katya. I see not a suitor but, instead, a hungry man walking away from a meal with a look of shame on his face."

❧

After only two weeks, I have adapted quite well to both my secretarial responsibilities and the routine farm chores. Just like in Minnesota, the fall harvest is one of the busiest times for farm work. Tasks are assigned each morning, and everyone attends to them with both vigor and zest. The robust garden maintains all the vegetables needed in the community year round. And the apple orchards and milking cows both provide a source of revenue for much-needed supplies, such as tools and dry goods.

Maria has been kind enough to present me with a number of *sarafans* dresses, each one more colorful than the last. While storing my western clothing, I wondered when I should ever have use for them again. My bad tooth is something else I should like to store away. The pain has disappeared since my arrival in Russia, but even though there is no more pain, over the past several weeks, I have begun to notice its subtle deterioration. On two recent occasions, I've felt fragments on my tongue. Prior to leaving France, a kind, elderly doctor friend of Auguste obliged my request to examine it. He noted that it was, in fact, breaking down and that it should fall out completely over time, although it would most likely not be replaced by a "permanent" tooth. An extraction would prove both difficult and painful, so he recommended allowing it to take its normal course.

Andre proves, at times, to be another source of irritation. I find his teasing both childish and entertaining. I sometimes wonder if I am back in school, where some of the boys were relentless with their incessant teasing.

"Why do you wear that?" he asked the other day, referring to my *kokoshnik* headdress. "You wear it like a foreigner."

I do not respond to his jibes, nor do I continue wearing the headdress, as I do find it awkward fitting. I've since worn my hair either down or in a ponytail, which, I feel, leaves me with a piece of individuality as a westerner.

"Good," said Andre just this morning. "The old customs have lost their meaning. Women with beautiful hair should let their hair flow down around their shoulders while the ends dance in the breeze."

*October 1900*

A ruling was announced this morning, and it was decided the two orphans that were deposited at the estate last week will stay on in the community. It was further decided that a childless couple shall be allowed to take them into their care. During a gathering, the older boy told of how his parents had been lost in a fire and their only relatives, an aunt and uncle, are too old to attend to their needs.

Many of the women find them endearing, as do I, but the question of whether they would remain was left to the men.

Some members believe they should be returned to the province from which they had come, but many agreed that such an endeavor would only prove fruitless, believing they would not have been brought all this way otherwise. No one gave a second thought to the suggestion that they be brought to the orphanage in Tula.

One man had suggested we consult the count on this matter, but Misha said that the count has entrusted us to make all decisions regarding the community and forbids himself from interfering. No man has a right to single himself out as a leader, but Misha is considered by many to be the unspoken head of the community.

The meeting had gone long into the evening as the women fawned over the two boys. A part of me had wished to adopt them forthright, but since I am a single woman, I am less qualified than those women who are married.

I now remember the mother that will never be. Ella's wish to marry and raise a family strikes a nerve, warming the back of my neck with unresolved restitution. I manage this new bout of guilt and anxiety with a notion that has eluded me all my life. I ask myself why it is that I would not make a good wife? A good mother?

❧

*February 1901*
Misha greets me with a wave of the hand while he splits logs with a great deal of aggression. The heavy blows coincide with each cloud of breath that floats then quickly vanishes above his cap. Today the master has been excommunicated by the Russian Orthodox Church. Misha tells me he is confused and believes it does not bode well for Yasnaya Polyana.

"But, Misha," I ask, "how can the count's excommunication be of concern? Are you not of the same mind as he?"

"Forgive me," he says with a smile. "These old rituals are not easy to leave behind."

I force a smile, gathering the cut wood in my arms, and think about him as a young child partaking in the rituals of the church and how impressionable he must have been, like me at that age.

"What about you, Nora?" He is almost breathless. "What do you think of this business?"

I ponder but a moment and explain, "I think of my own Lutheran upbringing. There was much I didn't understand as a child. The count's writings have given me a better understanding of what is good and proper in the world. Don't you agree?"

"Yes, I do," he answers. "But it is such a strange thing to learn that the count is no longer part of the Church. At least, when he was waging a battle against the clergy, I could feel that our little part of the world was still a part of the whole. But now..." He shrugs.

I understand what Misha means, and I too feel it, though not as strong. I think about the many years the peasants have entrusted themselves to the Church and how they were willing servants to the count all those years, as that is what had been prescribed. And once the count began to practice his own ideas of morality, the bind between peasantry and Church began to unwind.

Maria is walking toward us. "Nora, would you please help with the dinner?"

"But of course."

"And what has this old man been filling your head with?"

"Silence, woman! This is a dark day."

"Dark day!" Maria begins to laugh while wiping her hands against the sides of her dress. "Is it darkness when the people say, 'See! There he goes!' while pointing to the count this morning?"

"So the trouble begins," says Misha with sadness.

"Trouble? There is no trouble, old man. Just this morning, as he walked down the road, the people were offering him praise and gratitude."

"What's this?" I ask.

"No one pointed an accusatory finger at him," continues Maria. "No one rebuked him. He is treated like a saint."

"Blasphemy!" Misha snaps. "The count is not a saint, old woman. And anyone that claims he is blasphemies."

"Misha," I plead. "Don't you see? This is a good thing. This is part of the new life we shall all live someday soon. As the count changes the beliefs of the people, we become closer to living the new life."

As Maria and I walk off, I look back at Misha, now deep in thought. And as he readies the axe, I hear him mutter, "What does God care? It is but an old man cutting wood."

❦

A few days have passed uneventfully since the count's excommunication from the Church. While Misha and I make milk deliveries to the villages on the way to Tula, we are confronted by a group of villagers. There is a great deal of shouting; the word *blasphemers* stands out the loudest.

I had fallen under the false belief that the citizens of the surrounding communities were in agreement with the count's teachings. But this is only the case for the peasantry. The local authorities and businessmen are not of the same mind.

I listen as Misha speaks on behalf of the community and conclude his elderly voice commands respect.

"We'll have no more deliveries from Yasnaya Polyana," says a man, evidently the village elder.

"Does the milk offend you?" I note a subtle sarcasm in Misha's elderly tone.

"It does if it is from the estate of Count Tolstoy."

"Very well. I will inform my master that you no longer require his milk and have seen fit to receive your milk from a far holier land, shall I? Perhaps from heaven itself?"

"A debate regarding milk is not necessary, Mikael Popovich. More to the point is the trouble that will come once the tsar decides he will no longer put up with the heretical behavior of your master."

"Dear brothers, should we spend our time in worries regarding the tsar or make the most of each day under the guidance of God's teachings?"

"That is enough already, old man. Come away, everyone, and leave this old man to his deliveries. It is a fool who wastes his time trying to make a point to a fool."

As the men disburse and we continue on our way, I ask Misha his secret in diffusing the situation before it can even begin to boil. "You seem to have changed your attitude about these matters."

"The count's teaching of non-resistance to violence has its place, even among these good, though misguided, gentlemen. And besides, I think I grow less nervous with age when confronted with sticky situations."

The cool morning air along with our encounter gives me a sense of both exhilaration and dread. I am not one to back down from a fight, but now I begin to realize that I need not wind myself up any longer, for the true course of man is to resist these desires to strike back at evil.

"My concern now," begins Misha, interrupting my thoughts, "is the persecution that will be reaped upon the people from the tsar's military and secret police. And the Church knows its place. But as the saying goes, 'prayers for the tsar and blows for the people.'"

"How do you mean?"

"It is from past knowledge that I speak, child. The current tsar and the tsars before him have always resorted to intimidation and torture to keep the people from rising. But the master has taken up the common man's cause. He shall see us through to the promised land. But it will not be easy and will require courage and steadfastness."

I want to share with Misha the work I am doing on behalf of the count, but Mr. Kenworthy has sworn me to secrecy. And as long as both the tsar and the Church are inflamed by the count's writings and speeches, I am compelled to hold my tongue.

"Misha, you must tell me more about your home."

"You change direction in conversation as tactlessly as a bull let out to pasture," he says with a smile. I have no response for him and, instead, look ahead, down the street as we near our next delivery stop.

"Mine was a village of circus people."

I look at him. He reads my confused look instantly.

"Watch me." We stop in front of the merchant store for which we find ourselves on the other side of the village. He then steps down from the wagon and takes from the side compartment four packets of butter and begins to juggle them.

I laugh with delight. "You are very good, Misha."

"This is nothing. There are people from my village who could do more interesting tricks, some even dangerous."

"But how did you come to be in a circus?"

"My homeland is where the Russian National Circus was begun many years ago. You should go to Moscow sometime to see it."

As I help Misha unload our delivery, I cannot help but think about the circus that had been caught up in the tragedy of New Richmond less than two years ago.

⚜

It is late spring, and today is a day of rest that begins quite strangely. As we gather for breakfast, a new face appears before us. I quickly realize Andre is clean-shaven. I can't help but smile.

"Welcome, stranger," I say.

"Good morning." He sits down across from me.

His cheeks and neck are reddish, either from the close shave, embarrassment, or both. His brown eyes appear less piercing and softer against his dark eyebrows. A smile would give him the appearance of contentment. But, instead, its absence only provides a look of cautiousness.

After breakfast, I watch Andre walk outside with the other men while I help with the cleaning up.

Katya creeps up alongside me. "You have a mischievous look this morning, Nora."

"Am I really so obvious?"

She follows me outside.

The wind is blowing cold from the north. The thick, rainless clouds drift quickly across the sky. I imagine the world rotating south to north rather than west to east, bending the tree tops from the change in gravitational pull.

There are groups of men engaged in lively discussions all round the open square. Katya and I walk past them and down the path leading to the main road. The tall birches provide a break from the strong winds. I find Katya's company at times tiresome, as she seems limited in her knowledge and experiences, even though she is ten years older than I. She often asks me the same questions. "Did you see the count today? What does he write about? Do you hear him and his wife quarreling?"

She now asks me, "Are you aware that the countess threatens to move to Moscow?"

"Again?" I ask. "That is hardly news around here."

"True. But it is said that she has grown weary of all the disciples that constantly drop in unannounced."

"Then, yes, she should move away if she finds this tiresome."

"Do you ever notice anyone repeatedly visiting while you are working?"

"Goodness, Katya. I cannot say as I have noticed. Perhaps you should apply for a post in the household so that you may be more directly involved with the affairs of the count and his wife."

"I'm sorry, Nora, to be so inquisitive, but I find them to be a very interesting couple."

"Yes. The countess provides a great deal of excitement, but why pester me with these inquiries? The affairs of a husband and wife are of no concern to me."

I imagine how to avoid Katya and her annoying questions in the future without appearing rude.

*August 1901*
The summer has been both warm and rainy. The community has been blessed with good crops and a fine garden. It is the beginning of the harvest, and everyone is enduring the long days with a sense of contentment and oneness with the land. I have toiled along with the others, and our efforts have been fruitful. This should be enough to give me satisfaction and peace, but I feel there is something missing.

My sister, Ida, writes to me of her wedding and marriage. There is much happiness in her words. I can't help but feel envious. She has taken a simpler path than I. She has always been our mother's daughter, more so than I.

I grab a handful of dirt and squeeze it tightly in my hand. I watch it sift through my fingers and imagine how time and youth place such a burden on one to make decisions.

"You read too much, Nora," Andre says over his shoulder while swathing the hay. I have fallen behind in bundling the little stacks of hay.

"I read only what I want, which is enough. How can that be too much?"

"Your letter from home, you read it already twice before today."

"For you to know that, you must be spying on me."

"I spy you not working, but, instead, reading. That is what I spy."

I have finally come to a crossroads. I find myself falling for Andre. I am mesmerized by his boyish good looks. The sight of his etched shoulders rocking against the warmth of the countryside moves me in a way I know I shall find reminiscent in my old age. He makes me feel as though I am back at home in Minnesota, where the daily chores, good meals shared with family, and the closeness to God is palpable and is all that matters.

I have felt my inner-woman evolve over the past two years, but I have kept it in check for the sake of my purity. I have succeeded in rebuffing temptations laid upon me. Tristan desired my heart. Auguste wanted me for his passion. And Cassandra longed for compassion. There had been no pressure. But now a surge of my own creation begins to spiral out of control within me.

I toss a pebble at Andre's back. He ignores me, so I toss another.

"If you are not going to help, maybe you should go back to the village and read some more."

"I will help." I take the scythe from Andre and begin swathing with excessive vigor. The hay flies all around me, landing on my sweaty arms and in my hair. I am like a tornado creating its own path.

"What are you doing!" Andre shouts at me.

"I am working, because that is what we are all about here, work and nothing else."

"Stop now," he begs me. "You are either upset or crazy."

"How can you tell, Andre?" I stand before him, feigning puzzlement. "Are you a reader of emotions?"

"Come and sit. Is it your letter that has upset you?"

I ponder his question and begin to piece together the things that are upsetting me. Yes, the letter from Ida upsets me. The distance I am from home upsets me. The cruelties of the world that force the creation of a place such as Yasnaya Polyana upset me. But what upsets me most, I tell Andre. "Your lack of emotion is most upsetting to me, Andre."

"I don't understand what I have done to upset you."

"You do nothing, Andre, to inspire friendship between us. And that, I find most upsetting."

"Of course, we are friends."

"We may be friends, but we are not friendly."

He looks at me, understanding my meaning. "It is not proper."

"Who says?"

"The master has written…"

"Written that friendship is not acceptable?"

"Written that men and women revolve in separate worlds."

"Now you speak in platitudes, Andre. Can't you speak your own mind?"

"Nora, you have been here almost a year, and I believe you understand why you are here and why I am here and why we are all here."

"I believe there is a noose around the neck of this place, choking the feelings and emotions of all who live and work here."

"You are talking rot. I do not feel a noose around my neck."

Suddenly, I wrap my arms tightly around his arms and back and kiss him softly. He winces, but does not try to break my hold.

"Do you feel my arms around you, Andre?"

"Nora," he says, pausing. I can feel his hands lightly against my lower back. Then he returns my kiss with one of his own, equally soft. I press my lips hard against his. I feel my knees weaken as my mind begins to race with the centrifugal force of an anxious wind-mill, parsed by glimpses of things from my past telling me "No, Nora, no."

Finally, I think of nothing else except a desire welling up in me as we help each other to the ground. We both kneel, holding each other tightly, kissing as though we are in a place where rules are unheard of and all that matters is a truth bound by an embrace.

Time stands still as my mind absorbs this new sensation, the rhythm of lovers. I look beyond the blue eternity high above me. *There are no eyes,* I tell myself. *No one is watching.*

Suddenly it is ended, and I hear my heart beating like an overwound clock and feel the earth beneath me as I watch Andre quickly stand and walk off in the direction of the setting sun, leaving me lying in the field. I begin to feel overwhelmed with shame and guilt. It feels like I have just unveiled the true nature of who I am. I am back in Paris with Cassandra at the Moulin Rouge, dancing with reckless abandon, intoxicated and carrying on as though it were my last day on earth.

My tongue reaches to touch the remaining fragments of my last infant tooth, easily wiggling it back and forth until it finally dislodges. I spit at the dirt. I can now clearly see what I have been struggling with for the past several years. It looks like a small piece of bone, like something from a miniature archaeological dig. But I know it is more than that. It is the last of my innocence. And now, like my virginity, it lay on the ground, exposed and dirty.

During breakfast the following morning, Andre barely looks at me, causing my shame to increase tenfold. It is the Sabbath, and this only intensifies my feelings of immorality.

I am unable to eat and wait outside for Maria to walk with me to attend the morning services. It's pointless for me to attempt to hide my problems from her. Her insightfulness reminds me of my mother's premonitions and multiple sets of eyes. I believe God and I shall always be in close contact, with such strong maternal go-betweens linking the line of communication. "What ails you, Nora?"

"It's nothing. I just need a dose of spiritual cleansing."

"Have you had trouble with Andre?"

"It's of a personal nature." Maria smiles, seeing that I'm not intending to be rude but, rather, private, a somewhat rare commodity here at the estate.

A welcome distraction follows the services. The count, in his good nature and generosity, sends around the estate a wagon filled with ice, along with various flavors of syrups to make ice cones.

"The count has a craving for an ice cone today," explains a woman, a servant from the house of Tolstoy. She accompanies the wagon driver on a trek around the estate.

"But how did he gather so much ice on such short notice?" I ask.

"He is the count," says the driver. "He has his ways."

"Are you the American?" asks the woman.

"I'm Nora."

"And I am Olga. We rarely see you, as you are always so busy in the other end of the mansion. Would you like to come along with us to help distribute along the countryside?"

"I would love that very much."

I explain to Olga she need not instruct me on how to make an ice cone, as it is a familiar treat from back home.

After serving all the children and most of the adults, I tell Misha, "Don't be afraid. Do you see how the children are not afraid?"

"It is a children's delight." He waves off the whole affair with both timidity and curiosity.

"It is for grownups as well, old sir." Olga hands him a cone of ice with red syrup.

First Misha smells and then licks it.

"Afraid of ice, old man?" asks the driver. "Haven't you ever tasted the snow in the winter?"

"Quiet, Kolya," Olga scolds. "Are you so experienced in the ways of the world that nothing frightens you?"

"Of course. I am *always* weary of the quick tongue of a female."

Olga laughs as she gets back aboard the wagon and then helps me up.

The three of us speak of many things as we travel from one little community to the next. I ask what it is like to live in the home of the count and his wife.

"Most days are rather uneventful," says Olga, "and then there are days when there is complete chaos."

"Most recently yesterday," adds Koyla.

"Yes," continues Olga. "There are days when one imagines the entire house collapsing because of the battle between husband and wife. They are both equally stubborn. He demands peace and quiet so that he may work, and she demands his constant attention."

I cannot hide the look of bewilderment on my face. "Let us just say," Olga concludes, "they are a very energetic couple."

"With all the visitors," I suggest, "it is a wonder the count is able to get any work done."

"And from visitors come spies."

"Really? I've heard of these attempts."

"You should know of one such spy."

"I assure you, I know of none."

"The former dairy maiden, Katya, was one such spy. I had heard you were friends."

"Katya!" I am shocked to hear this news but think back to the time of her sudden disappearance. Misha explained she had departed without so much as a good-bye and had attributed it to a family emergency. But now this news sheds light on the many questions she had regarding the count and his wife.

"It is the count's youngest daughter, Alexandra, who revealed Katya as a spy," Olga continues. "She is the only child of the count's who is a true Tolstoyan."

"I have heard that she is very devoted."

"She is devoted, yes, to her father, but not so much to her mother."

"I think it is the duty of a child to be equally devoted to both parents."

"This household is different."

"Very true," Kolya adds.

I can't help but think *different* meant *unhappy,* while remembering the opening sentence of *Anna Karenina*.

*October 1901*

The community is apt to give thanks to the heavens often and for any number of reasons. The harvest is not one of the lesser reasons. There is a feeling of accomplishment and a strong belief God has provided our every need for the upcoming winter.

There is a milky twilight, the kind made for those in love, and inside the community hall, the autumnal celebration finds everyone jovial. Unfortunately, I can't find the energy to be caught up in the festivities. In addition to the not-so-distant memory of Ella, I am now troubled with the burden of carrying Andre's child. We have not been alone together since our time in the field. Since then, everyone has been engaged in either strenuous labor or somber meditation.

Maria offers me hot cider and begs me to join her and Misha in a *troika*. I explain that I have never been much of a dancer and how she would be putting her and Misha's toes in danger. But now I spy Andre standing across the hall, scanning the crowd. I am sure he is looking for me, so I make my way toward him.

Andre hands me a pamphlet and tells me to read it for the sake of my immortal soul. I smile at him, to which he gives no notice, and then he turns to leave.

"Where are you going?" I shout above the music, but he disappears from the hall and into the night.

I walk slowly across the dance floor as the jubilant atmosphere pounds my state of awkwardness into dust. It is too important a message to leave until later. Now I rush from the hallway before it is even midnight; I find myself alone with the pamphlet. As I read by candle-light, I search for a pronouncement of Andre's love in between the lines. But the more I read about the aging, jealous husband and his growing hatred toward his wife and her lover, the more I realize Andre's intention is, in fact, to provide a moral lesson. I am saddened by this story, not only because it provides no redemption in character, but neither does it give me an indication as to Andre's true feelings toward me.

I scour the estate in search of Andre. The possibilities of his location are few in number for this time of day. Perhaps the hut he shares irregularly with three others or in the stables grooming the horses, but most likely, solitude in the barn with a book lent from the count's library.

Finding him there, I confront him regarding his suggestion that I am the woman in the *Kruetzer Sonata*. "Why else would you give me this?" I demand.

"The point of the story is for us both to acknowledge that what happened between us was an abomination."

"Do you favor yourself an equal to the count?"

"What do you mean?"

"I have heard the stories told of his illegitimate off-spring smattered about the estate."

"Are you saying…" He pauses, realizing what I have revealed to him. He takes on the airs of indifference. "The count's affairs have nothing to do with ours."

Hearing Andre use the word *ours* gives me a small bit of hope that we can come together for the sake of our unborn child.

"So you're saying your child is an abomination?"

His face goes blank, and then it seems to change to that of distrust. "This is one of your womanly traps, Nora Nelsovna, and I won't be tricked into playing your games."

"You'll see this spring what game is to be played."

"Even so, it may be someone else's."

I slap his face without hesitation. "It is as if you had no part in what happened. And that is the worst part of this piece of trash." I hold the pamphlet up in his face. "That there is condemnation for the wife, but nothing but the beating of the chest for the supposed protagonist, protesting at the top of his lungs that he has been corrupted by the she-devil and seeks only forgiveness for his transgression."

"I think you missed the very essence of the piece, Nora Nelsova," he says, again addressing me all too formally.

"Don't be so ridiculous, Andre. Don't act as if we have not been intimate. It is insulting. And I think it is *you* who have missed the point of the tale, unless you agree that you are the essence of the wife's lover."

"I gave you the pamphlet not to illustrate similarities between its characters and our relationship, but rather to show that there can be nothing but trouble between a man and a woman when they choose to go against the master's teachings."

Again he uses the word *our*, but this time I find it offensive. "You speak so highly of the master on this subject," I respond, "when all along you appear to dismiss his other teachings. I shouldn't wonder if this is more a sign of a coward than a man of conviction."

He appears to shudder at this charge, and I can't help but think there is a spark of truth in what I have said.

"As such," I continue, "I wonder if you are even worthy of fatherhood."

"Nora," he begins to plead, "if you are truly with child, then I think it would be best if you made your way back to America to be with family."

"In God's name," I sigh. "Is this the universal response of weak men when confronted with moral dilemmas?"

Andre does not appear to understand my rhetorical question, but I am in no mood to explain the convenient suggestion made by Soren regarding Ella's situation. In fact, the thought of Ella provides me with instant resolve with regard to Andre.

"I will take your suggestion under advisement." My voice is laced with sarcasm.

He sighs with utter contempt. "Think clearly about this and know that I will be discussing your circumstances with Mr. Kenworthy."

"This is a private affair," I protest.

"Nevertheless, you have placed us both in a very compromising position."

❧

*February 1902*

I have been dismissed by Mr. Kenworthy. He does not give me an explanation, but it feels obvious to me he knows I am with child. His whole demeanor, as well as those he speaks on behalf of, swirls around me like a cloud of hypocrisy. I have never given a second thought to the count's numerous bastards, but just now, their spirits seem to skulk about the room. It is all I can do to maintain my composure while I bite my tongue.

I bolt from the mansion, leaving the front door ajar.

Misha and Maria are the only ones I can depend on. Sensing my despair, they help me set up a home in an abandoned hut on the edge of the woods. What is funny is I have become an outcast within a community of outcasts.

"You know this is not necessary, Nora." Maria looks out the door to make sure Misha is not within earshot.

"Of course, it's necessary. I am ruined."

"You are with child. And having seven of my own, I can tell you it is far from ruin. Who is the father? He needs to take his part in this."

"A coward. It would be better that you liken my condition to that of the Virgin Mary."

"Nora, yours is a tongue that waggles blasphemy without first thinking. I can see that you don't believe what you say, but others may not understand." Her scolding turns into comfort as she holds my face in her hands and smiles. "Be patient. This coward you speak of, his conscience will get the better of him over time."

"Will she really stay here alone?" I hear Misha ask as Maria steps out the door.

"She'll not be alone. God will keep her."

I have become, yet again, a kept woman. Only this time I am burdened.

*March 1902*
I now live with a great deal of anxiety of my own creation. I have fallen into an abysmal state. At times, I should like to blame my parents for having sheltered me from the realities of the world, while at other times, I consider the count's teachings as a muddling force to how I have fallen from grace. But in the end, I always realize it is my own free will which has condemned me.

The thought of free will reminds me of my conversations with Tristan not so long ago. I think about how I have strayed so far from my upbringing, far from the security of my small, rural life, only to find myself lost in the uncertainty of a far-away, rural life.

While sitting on a bench outside, I see far down the road the figure of a traveler carrying a large backpack approaching. My heart leaps at the thought of a visitor, but I imagine it is merely someone passing by. The closer he comes, the more I think about who it can be in such a remote part of the estate. I recall Misha explaining how the count is known to venture about the estate, mingling with the peasants, talking and working alongside them.

"Hello," I say.

"You are the painter from America?" he asks.

"I paint, though I am hardly renowned."

"I have seen your works and enjoy them. You see much detail in the Russian landscape. It is as though you are from the country or at least possess the vision of God." He smiles softly through his long beard and moustache.

"I was born and raised in the country. Someday, I should like to return to capture on canvas the same things I have captured in this land."

"How strange it must be to come so far, only to realize you should never have left your home."

I ignore the suggestion that I don't belong in Russia.

"That did not sound right," he says.

I smile, imagining how such a prophetic writer could manage to trip over his tongue at this very moment.

"Don't mind my ineptitude," he continues, "but the true reason I am here is that I have brought these things for you."

I take note of the several canvases and pouches of colored powders and numerous brushes.

"I should feel honored," I say, "but I can't help but feel that it is not my conscience you are attempting to relieve of such a heavy burden."

The count does not reproach me but, rather, gives me a look of both understanding and sincerity, so I continue. "Besides painting, I used to translate some of your writings until I was dismissed."

"If you'll permit me to confess," he says with sternness, "I have much in this old life to apologize for. I'm afraid I have not carried my burden well. See to it that you do not do likewise."

"Please don't think me impertinent, but I think I have come to believe that much of your preachings are both strident and elusive in the application for the common people."

"Well said. I suppose that is why it comes down to the individual, standing alone before God, to make the ultimate decision." He chuckles. "Whatever that choice may be."

I feel empty inside as I stare into his dark, empty eyes. The quietness of my surroundings is no longer familiar. Even my unborn child is still. It is as if we are waiting for the world to finally crash and put an end to it all.

"Please be safe. And remember where your roots are. In the end, they may prove to be the closest bond you have to the truth."

He starts walking back down the road in the direction he came. When he falls below the distant horizon, I kick the satchel, watching its contents scatter across the road.

*April 1902*

I begin a painting of Misha's grandchildren seated on one of the mares. I have found an ideal spot, suitable at the best time of day. The morning clouds have all disappeared, so I am free to take full advantage of the good lighting.

I intend to capture the simple life of children and animals in an earthy landscape, absent of the lushness of the summer season. I am close to giving birth, and it is my desire to put to canvas the memory of this day. Without the presence of my own siblings, I consider Misha's grandchildren to be the siblings of my unborn child, full of innocence against the harshness of the Russian springtime. I wish to convey perseverance and respect for the land, as this is where my child will grow up.

I aim the brush with a clumsy wave around my big belly. I think of my homeland so far off as I splatter a gray-brown mix against the horizon and then pull it into the foreground with a fading lightness that echoes a truth dissolving into a lie. This is a dark day.

*May 1902*

Maria wipes my forehead. I can't look in her eyes as she comforts me. My breathing is labored, but that is to be understood. She has been by my side since early this morning, and now the late afternoon sun breaks through the cloud cover and a beam of light squeezes through a crack in the hut, striking the edge of the bed like an hour hand, reminding me of this long day's chore.

The ebb and flow of birthing continues for several hours. I am no longer panicked but resolve to see this burden through to its end. The tedium is similar to the depopulating of an apple tree by several peasants. The end goal is near, as due diligence has taken hold until finally the last ripe apple has been plucked. Only here, I labor alone, and the picking is in the hands of God, who shall decide when this child shall enter this world.

I sense prying eyes in the room, and I see out of the corner of my eye darkness leaning heavy on the window. A moment later, both Maria and I hear a thud outside. I look toward the window and notice it is not so dark after all.

"What could that be?" she wonders and then gets up.

As she opens the door, I am about to tell her to be careful but, instead, shout her name. "Maria!"

She quickly returns to my side as I feel my youth giving way to the momentum of new life.

⚜

*July 1902*
Today was lecture day. Both Maria and Misha begged with persistence that I return to the community.

Misha spoke with increased seriousness. "You are becoming known as the strange American woman who has hermitized herself in a foreign land."

Maria pleaded how much care and support my child and I would find back in the community.

"See how my little Teodor cries?" I asked. "See how he is on the verge of a tantrum? I need to exorcise myself of a tantrum seething for months now. I have been in a place where I'm not sure what to believe."

"I might not find the desire to help you this coming winter." Misha's attempt at coercion is weak at best. His words are made of stone, but his heart is as soft as the gift he has made for my baby—leather boots.

The brush feels foreign to my hand. Maybe it is because of who it is from and where I am. I attempt to paint a portrait of Ella from memory, as I find myself more and more longing for my homeland. It feels like the only way I can reach out to my past.

It is lonely here with a child but no father. It's been so long since I have thought of Ella. I realize now that is a bad thing. Even in death, her memory and my little Teodor are the purest things I have to cling to in this world.

*October 1902*
Dusk joins me in my quiet isolation. I hear a knock at the door. Teodor, his infant chatter interrupted, looks into my eyes. His are filled with curiosity—mine, concern.

I open the door a crack, allowing the cool night air in. Andre stands outside, hat in hand.

"Why are you here, Andre? Do you require the warmth of a woman now that the cold approaches?"

"You will need help with getting through the winter. I will reside in the barn."

"It's not so simple," I begin to explain. "I have in my arms a child without a father."

"I will take care of both you and the child. Is that not simple enough?"

"We have Misha and Maria to look after us."

"They may not always be around to help, such as when the snow obstructs their path."

I look at Andre, waiting for him to give me the right answer as to why I should allow him to stay on.

"Nora, I have nowhere else to go," he stammers. "I have no place to work. I have been discovered as a spy for the tsar's police."

I think about this. I try to imagine Andre as a traitor to the new life. It seems to make sense. However, I can hardly sympathize with him, as I know my banishment is far more unjust than his. But all at once I feel compassion for him. No matter the burdens I carry, I feel I am still graced by the mercy of God, but Andre, on the other hand, is a lost soul, indeed. I begin to believe I have truly taken advantage of his reserved nature.

"Yes. You may stay in the barn, but the cold would be unbearable." I cannot live with myself if the father of my child were to freeze to death only paces away. "It would make more sense for you to sleep inside."

I am the sort of person who forgives easily, like a needy dog sniffing at the fingertips for acceptance from the hand that has recently struck its snout. Unlike the dog, I should know better. If I'm none the wiser, it is most likely due to something innate to my nature or perhaps attributable to my passive and tolerant heritage. "We are not so special," my mother once told me. I had just done something that caused me to be prideful, but her remark stopped me cold as I considered what she meant. I was too ashamed to ask. At first, I felt as though I were being scolded. But then I thought how often my parents had made the point of instructing all their children not to think so high above our own heads. I remember then thinking of the eyes of God staring down upon me. So strange how something so trite can leave a lasting impression on one's worldview.

The simple life further accentuates my predilection toward the submissive, the bowing down to authority in all its manly forms. Andre is the backbone of our little hovel, and I am the nurturer. He makes the strenuous daily trek to the barn to milk our lone cow. He chops and stacks the wood that will keep us warm through the long winter. The simple dedication by which he goes about these responsibilities overshadows the darkness that pervades the hearts of all men. I have fallen for his dedicated and rhythmic strokes in these endeavors, just I did two summers ago while he turned hay into stock.

I know my place in this world is equal parts necessity, regret, and ingratitude. I have taken up the cause of redemption, but there are times I wish I could turn back the clock and start anew, perhaps adjusting this moment or that in hopes of redirecting the course of my own history. Alas, all is as God intended. I cheerfully accept my comeuppance.

*January 1903*
We are buried in two feet of new snowfall. There is nothing for us to do but while away the day, staring into the corners. I am tired of longing for the home of my youth.

I stop my knitting and watch Andre bob a little ball tied to a stick above Teodor, whose laughter is filled with enthusiasm while his little fingers flex and grip. I begin to ponder the man who was once an infant. "I know almost nothing of your youth."

Andre stops playing with Teodor and gazes into the light of the stove. He tells me of his tragic youth, how he lost his father to the coal mine when he was only ten. He took his father's place, but his mother fretted for his safety. And because he could not match his father's efforts and pay, he and his mother and sister were forced to move to Stavropol, where all three of them lived and worked in the factory that made soap. You would think it would have been a clean place to work, but in fact, the conditions were terrible and the hours long. Andre watched as his sister became very sick one winter as a result of the constant change of temperature in the factory. Many others grew ill as well. There was an outcry by a few for better conditions, and for their efforts, they were beaten and dismissed. The workers endured the harsh conditions for as long as they could until, one day, they organized a strike and were summarily crushed by the local dragoons. Andre lost both his mother and sister that day. He ran away from the city in fear, believing that the tsar's police would be out to kill him as well.

He tells me of the past ten years, migrating from one province to the next, always in search of finding a place where he could belong.

I am afraid for Andre, as he is a man who has no clear identity. I try to convince him that he is a father to a wonderful little baby boy and that he should take great pride in this.

"Since I am confessing all things to you, Nora, I should also inform you that the work you were doing for the count was a subterfuge."

"What do you mean?"

"I was tasked by the local police to keep track of your activities. And once that became known to Kenworthy, he had no use for you as a decoy."

"But the translations were intended to be smuggled out of the country for foreign publication."

"Kenworthy was using another source less known to the local police to manage that work and to smuggle out of the country. I think you were conveniently employed to draw attention away from that person. At the time, I thought it quite obvious, but I allowed the local police to imagine they knew better."

Now I think that maybe I had been dismissed not because I was bearing a child, but because my services were no longer useful to the count. Either way, I find the circumstance apprehensible.

"I am sorry, Nora. I know your intentions were of the noblest kind and mine not so much so."

*April 1903*

The spring thaw brings with it a chance for renewal. Misha visits us less frequently during the winter but arrives today with supplies. As I watch from the doorway, he and Andre embrace and speak lively; I can tell that he no longer distrusts the former spy.

Misha walks over to see Teodor in my arms.

"And how is the little man today?" He offers Teodor a rough finger.

"He has endured the long winter like a true Norwegian."

"You mean like a true Russian," he corrects me with a chuckle intended for Teodor.

"As you wish." I smile. "You must come in for some fresh-made bread."

"None for me. I can only visit a moment. I have news," he says most seriously. "There is a teaching post available at the school. It has been agreed by the elders that you should return to the community to teach."

"I don't understand, Misha," I say, half interested. "There was so much ill will toward me last summer, my certainty that I should never again set foot in the community was pronounced."

"Nora has a new life out here." Andre speaks with confidence as he strolls up and alongside me and Teodor.

Misha ignores Andre's words. "And we could use another hand in the field."

"Now *I* don't understand," says Andre.

"Nora, you were never told to leave the community. You left on your own, did you not?"

"Yes, but that was because—"

"It is easier to speak of tolerance and forgiveness than it is to practice. We cannot all be nearly as perfect as the master." He smiles and begins to walk away.

Andre and I exchange looks of bewilderment.

"You will think about it, won't you?" he says to me and then looks to Andre. "And you too?"

"What do you make of that, Nora?" asks Andre.

"I make of it as the word of Christ himself spoken through the count."

"He is a queer one, indeed."

"He is a contradiction is what he is."

I think about my comment and realize I too am a contradiction. While I had spent all winter filled with anger toward the count and his peasant followers, I quickly feel this rush of compassion and forgiveness toward the lot of them. I am not so hopeless after all.

❦

*May 1903*
I have taken on the curriculum prescribed by the count himself, in which the teacher manages a controlled chaos. There are a number of peasant children varying in ages who are permitted to come to school whenever they choose and to learn whatever they want. Little Teodor lies quietly atop my desk, taking in all the sounds and sights before him.

I teach the little ones about the many different species roaming the earth and how they interact with each other. I draw pictures of animals from other parts of the world and encourage the children to do likewise. Many of them have never attempted to be so creative and are very apprehensive. I demonstrate for them how one must freely sketch based on personal interpretation.

The older children are more interested in learning about other parts of the world and the people and cultures. I engage them in philosophical discussions regarding the various types of religions and governments throughout the world. The count has made various study guides available to the numerous peasant schools throughout the estate, but I have no intention of influencing their freedom of thought. A small group of the older boys are seated along a bench on the far side of the room. I walk over to listen to their discussion and only interject a comment when I feel it is relevant and perhaps useful.

Andre is skeptical of my activities. "These are peasant children," he says. "What on earth can they do with such knowledge? They are wards of the count and will remain as such until all private property has been taken back by the people."

"Andre," I explain, "I know you are wise enough to understand that a nation is built on the backs of its poor and uneducated. It is the case in my own country. And now it is a great republic."

"Yes, due to your civil war. And that is what is needed here in Russia."

"I don't understand how you can say such things. It is as if you have learned nothing from the count's teachings. Perhaps," I begin to jest, "some time spent in the schoolroom would do you some good as well."

*January 1905*
I am in the third winter of my life in Russia. I have found happiness with a man and a child on a piece of land that reminds me of my youth. Most nights are very quiet, and I sometimes focus on the reflection of the flickering candle light in the window. Looking just beyond the darkness, I pretend my family is in a room on the other side. Everyone is asleep. The ties

to both past and present families provide comfort. As the count has written, it is the simple things that make life most rewarding. Strange to learn in this place that such was the case back home, half a world away.

⚜

The day starts out with the brilliant sunlight gleaming off the fresh snowfall for which Andre has fashioned a toboggan to pull little Teodor upon in circles around the field. I stand outside and throw snowballs as Andre draws near. I hide behind a post as he returns fire. Teodor's little hands gobble up as much snow as they can hold, and he joins me in throwing snowballs at his father.

Andre is a master of seasoning and provides a hardy soup of rutabaga, potatoes, and carrots for the mid-day meal.

Just as we are about to sit down to eat, Misha arrives unexpectedly and reports to us the tragedy of a fortnight ago, in which many factory workers protesting for their rights were killed by the tsar's military in front of the Winter Palace.

"They marched on the palace quietly," he says, "with a petition in one hand and a cross in the other."

"How many were killed?" Andre asks.

"Many." Misha shrugs. "Perhaps hundreds. Women and children as well."

"What will happen now?" I ask.

"There is talk of countrywide strikes and demonstrations."

"Then I shall journey to Tula to be beside my comrades."

"I beg you not to go too, Andre. You are needed here."

He paces the room. "It is as if history repeats itself." He is clearly angry and wishes to strike out against someone.

Misha explains how the count has petitioned the tsar to employ compassion and fairness in dealing with the workers.

Andre appears unimpressed. "The count manages the world's affairs from the comfort of his study."

"The count," says Misha, "is the same person who gave you sanctuary on his estate those years ago in spite of your treacheries."

Andre pauses and stares at Misha, apparently to rethink his position. But before he can respond, I plead, "Yes, Andre. This is business left to the persuasions of the count."

⚜

*July 1905*

The big pond on the estate has a communal canoe that Andre and I use to paddle about in with little Teodor during the warm seasons. There is a little pavilion on shore where we can take shelter from poor weather or just relax beneath the birch trees while picnicking. Sometimes we fall into a world of make believe, imagining we own the estate. This gives me a sense of luxury, living akin to a country lady while, at other times, I feel as though I am straying from my convictions. In the end, it seems like a trifle indulgence.

Today, as the azure sky begins to transcend into dusk, Andre maneuvers back to shore. As I step long toward the shore, holding my hefty Teodor in my arms, Andre asks if I mind pulling the canoe farther into shore. I look at him credulously.

"I'd prefer not getting my new boots wet," he says.

"Very well." I grab the bow and tug with great effort, only to tumble backward onto the ground. Teodor giggles while rolling out of my grasp and on to the ground. My cheeks begin to burn.

"I'm sorry, Nora." Andre holds a straight face, as is his usual demeanor. Should he even chortle, I'm quite certain I will give him praise for showing the least bit sign of emotion. But it is not in his nature, as I have grown to learn over the years.

I spy a rabbit staring at me as I lie prone. Teodor stands but does not see the little creature. "What are you looking at?" I ask. As I lift myself, I conclude I am probably a rare sight for our little lop-eared friend. "If you come across clumsy humans in the future, you should, no doubt, appear less quizzical," I say, reasoning with the little critter.

"Why did you make me do that, Andre?"

"As I said, I didn't want to get my boots wet." I see him smirk. "Besides, you are always going on about the equality of women, so I think you would approve of my encouraging you to assist me."

"Yes, but don't expect me to heft you up onto the backboard, as I'm sure I would incur an injury."

Just as I am about to give Andre credit for not increasing my embarrassment through either ridicule or laughter, he says, "The count is a clever man. He solicits the support of not only the men but the women by suggesting equality. Even the tsar is not clever enough to double his support with such a notion. It will surely end his reign in time."

I have heard of the count entertaining the notion of allowing the peasant women to join the All-Russian Union of Equal Rights for Women. Most believe the tsar has no intentions of entertaining women's rights, but several of the young women on the estate found the notion intriguing. I was not afraid to voice my opinion, which they found to be quite advanced in relation to their own. In a small and somewhat meaningless way, I became a lightning rod for debate on the subject. This, of course, was frowned upon by Andre.

"What do you find so offensive about women having the same rights as men?" I ask him.

"There are things that cannot be changed about the order of the world."

"Then you are saying a woman should remain subservient to her husband?"

He is silent. I seize the opportunity to instruct him. "Perhaps, if men hadn't kept women out of the sciences and arts for so many centuries, we would be less apt to make poor decisions when it comes to such important issues. As it stands, you'll have to afford us the mistakes we shall undoubtedly make while improving the world, in spite of the shape your lot has brought it to."

Andre and I say nothing more on the subject. I feel his silence indicates not agreement but just the opposite.

*November 1910*
The winter has just begun, and news of the master's passing spreads quickly throughout the countryside. I

think of the only time we shared a conversation. I now feel remorse for having not been more conciliatory and appreciative of the gifts he gave me and the manner in which he did so. Strangely, I imagined we were so much closer but now attribute such a feeling to his omnipresence throughout the country. His presence provided a sense of stability on the estate. I can't help but wonder what will become of us all.

There will be many mourners making the pilgrimage to Yasnaya Polyana to pay their respects to the master.

Although Ella is often in my thoughts, it's been ten years since I lost her. In that same time, I have buried two infant daughters. I try to imagine the four of them together in a kingdom where the saints dwell, fostering both peace and tranquility. I imagine Ella, so young and naïve, with my little girls on her lap, mistaking the master with his long, gray beard to be God himself.

*June 1913*
It is the third summer since the master's passing. Since then, the estate does not feel so organized or inspired, as there is a lack of leadership. The estate is managed by the countess, who, we are told, grows less tolerant in the face of pressure from the tsar and considers breaking from the old communal ways and joining a farm cooperative. The politics of it all escape me, but it is evident that the countess is willing to succumb to both state and church in these matters. This does nothing to encourage followers to come and, in fact, encourages those who have been here for years to depart. I hear of many leaving for the other similar-style communities

located on the periphery of Russia, places where the leaders of some dare to claim to be the second coming of Christ.

Misha, who now slowly walks with a cane round the estate, informs me that the countess is mostly concerned with her children's inheritance. She is attempting to find the right balance between the tsar's rule of law and her husband's beliefs, but even a blind man can see how fruitless the effort.

⚜

*August 1913*

As Andre and I are tilling a section of acreage near the master's burial site, I am startled by the sight of a stilted object among the rustling weeds just near the tree line. Its color is not an earth tone. As I draw near, the color appears mauve, and the material is cloth. I stop in my tracks, as I now think it is someone napping under the afternoon sun. But now there is an awkward bend to the position of the body part, a leg, that is visible, and the color turns from mauve to crimson as a cloud's shade passes. I slowly step forward to see the open eyes of Misha; he is lying on his back. There is a large red patch covering his white wool shirt. I am not so naïve to imagine he is still alive while staring up directly into the blinding sun. I begin to tremble and press myself to decide what to do next.

I walk slowly away from Misha and wave down Andre, who is working the far side of the field. He cannot see me, nor can he hear me, as I am unable to shout out to him. Finally, he hears my footsteps and turns round.

"What is wrong?"

"It is Misha. He is dead."

It is evening when we are visited by a local authority, who is accompanied by a member of the Ohkrana. After the two have conducted a preliminary assessment of both the body of Misha and the site where I had found him, they conclude there has been foul play.

"That was already understood," says Andre. "It is evident to anyone with eyes that he was run through with a cutlass."

"Andre." I am now nervous for our safety and wish he would not antagonize the investigators.

"Quite right, Andre Dimitrovich." The Ohkrana official, a man who holds himself in high esteem by way of a fine suit and aromatic hair tonic, appears to be searching Andre's face for clues. "How is it you know it was a cutlass that killed Mikhael Popovich?"

"I am former military. I am obviously familiar with such things."

I pull Andre toward me, but he stands steadfast, toe to toe with the official.

"And do you own such weaponry, Andre Dimitrovich?"

"I do not. I dispensed with it many years ago."

"And you would not be opposed to a search of your home?"

"Of course not."

The official instructs the local authority to begin conducting a search. The process feels more like a form of harassment than investigation, as everything in our home is turned over.

Nothing is found, and they proceed down the road.

The following day, as is custom, Misha is given a proper burial. Mirrors in every household are covered with black cloth so that his spirit will no longer be among the living. A large procession of the locals accompanies Misha's body from his home to the community hall. The hall is not large enough to accommodate all the people who come to pay their respects. I am instantly reminded of the gathering that accompanied the funeral of the master. Misha was a man who had lived, not as a famous writer or aristocrat, but rather as a common peasant. But even so, the love and respect he had earned over his life was as equally astounding as that of the master's.

Now a line has formed as people pass through the hall in a counter-clockwise manner, passing his body, either kissing or placing flowers on him as he lay in his coffin. From there, the procession continues to a nearby cemetery where many peasants of Yasnaya Polyana lay buried. Afterward, we all gather back at the community hall for vodka and food and to share stories about Misha's life. One man, a very old friend, speaks about a time when Misha and he and several others had spent days hunting a crazed bear that had been terrorizing the village for weeks. Many farms had been attacked by the bear and livestock killed and not eaten. A woman who had been out among the sheep was mauled and later died from her wounds. He spoke of the sadness that had accompanied the hunters as they tracked their quarry. Finally, when they had cornered the bear, Misha insisted on taking the kill shot. All agreed, as he was known as a marksman from his days of fighting during the Crimean War. We are told how he wished to help the bear find peace quickly, avoiding an agonizing death.

❧

For a fortnight, we find ourselves embroiled in a murder investigation in which the Ohkrana has given itself carte blanche in dealing with the matter. The whole thing reeks of conspiracy, as there is a grand effort to widely publicize the incident and to incriminate community members, thus discrediting the Tolstoyan concept of non-violence. An effort is made to include Andre, as he was the first man to arrive at the murder scene. Though my testimony provides an ample alibi, I believe, it is my American lineage that helps to dissuade the authorities from continuing in this direction.

The countess, referring to Misha as a loyal subject to the House of Tolstoy, wishes to bring the guilty parties to bear in the name of justice. Two new community members, transient, single men from the Caucuses, serve to expedite this process and are quietly imprisoned in Stavropol.

I am saddened by these events and decide it would be best for Andre, Teodor, and me to reside peacefully in our little section of the estate and to limit our social contact to that of attending the community church and the teaching of the school-aged children.

There are days I sense Andre's anguish. I believe there are times he feels he has squandered his life. It is Teodor that reminds him that there has been something God given that has made for a wonderful life here.

# Do Not Be Frightened

When you hear of wars and revolutions, do not be frightened. These things must happen first, but the end will not come right away.

Luke 21:9

*June 1914*

I have had the wonderful opportunity as a teacher to help inspire young minds. I have shared a life with a man who shares my love for our son. And I have done all this in a place that reminds me of my home. But nothing lasts forever. Teodor is twelve and Andre has decided to leave us to join the tsar's military to fight against the Germans. Teodor wants to join as well, but I forbid him. Even so, I begin to feel my little home on the edge of the estate begin to disintegrate. I busy myself by hanging the laundry.

"It is rather puzzling, Andre, that you choose to fight on behalf of the tsar after having been so repulsed by his aggression toward the common people for so many years."

"Don't be ridiculous. I would never fight for the dynasty but, rather, for Mother Russia." He stares past me, huffing and puffing. "You are not Russian, so how could you possibly begin to understand?"

"I've spent fourteen years of my life in this country. I brought a half-Russian child into this world. I've lived under the tenets of this country's most renowned writer. Am I not yet a little bit Russian?"

He bends over and picks up a handful of dirt. "A proper Russian knows when it is time to take up arms against the enemy for this."

"And what about the late count's teachings of non-resistance?"

"Such notions are for intellectuals and philosophers."

"But it is the better part of man and is something we should strive for."

"Have I not allowed you to instill these tenets in our son without interruption?"

"Yes."

"Then why, Nora, does he wish to come with me to fight?"

"It is merely a son's wish to be with his father. And I forbid him to go. We both know he is not old enough to fight."

"Yes. I agree." Andre kneels before Teodor, resting a hand upon his shoulder. "Son, I want you to stay here with your mother. Do you understand?"

Teodor gives his father a reluctant nod as I step behind him and place my own hands upon his shoulders.

⁂

It is all concluded. Andre has made his choice. He and several of the other men in the community will fight for the tsar in the event of war and have gone to Tula to enlist.

Teodor is crestfallen as his father walks down the road. I am not feeling the same emotion but instead begin to feel the last spark of my life is my son, who weeps while the figure of his father grows smaller and smaller.

Not even a month goes by before I concede my inability to content myself with Andre's absence. For the first time since arriving in Russia, I feel completely isolated and out of place, as the lines of borders become more accentuated by people retreating to their own tribes. And nothing speaks more ominously and loudly than the opinions of others as the threat of war looms.

I have had dollars and francs from my old life squirreled away all these years. I decide that my son and I should make our way back to Paris and, with the help of Auguste, God willing, back to America.

"But what about papa?" asks Teodor. "How will he find us?"

"We shall leave word along the way. If he is the father you imagine him to be, won't he seek us out?" His look says as much as had he said aloud, "I don't believe you."

I bid farewell to all my old friends and neighbors.

"Dear Nora," asks Maria, "what should we tell Andre when he returns?"

I look into her old gray-blue eyes. "If he returns, let him know he has broken my heart and I have taken our son away."

We apply at the US Embassy for visas. I tell my son his name is now Teodor Thorsen. He does not understand.

We're able to find safe conduct through Austria and into Switzerland. From there, we reach France.

❧

I find Auguste in his studio, seated. He does not hear us enter from behind. I see that he is holding the picture of his parents. I am amazed I still recall from so many years ago both the picture and its importance for Auguste.

"Auguste," I say softly.

He straightens to turn round.

"Are you dozing?" I ask, smiling with joy.

"Nora!" He stands up and sets the picture on the chair. We embrace.

He sees Teodor and then looks at me with a broad smile. "A son?"

"Oui, monsieur."

He makes tea, and we catch up. He tells of the great gains in the Parisian art world since my last visit and how he has fallen from the graces of the artists' community due to his allowing the commercialization of his art.

"I realize I am more a capitalist than a true artist. But enough about me. It has been a good decade for my former colleagues, particularly my Negro colleagues." He stammers while displaying his enthusiasm. "Paris has found its soul, but just at the wrong time. A new war, Nora, a reminder of the last one, the one France faired not so well in."

"I know little of wars, Auguste. I only know that I have come, selfishly, to seek your help in returning to America."

"I am afraid, Nora, you have arrived at a bad time. The entire city is mobilizing. There are rumors that any day now, the German army will march on France."

"That's terrible."

"I am just now packing my belongings."

"But where will you go?"

"I can't go to my villa to the northeast, as that is, no doubt, an area that will see much fighting."

"Where then? Will you leave the country?"

"Never! I will head south and see how long we can stave off the crushing wave of the Hun, even if it means guerilla warfare in the Pyrenees. Why don't you and your son come with me, Nora? In fact, I insist. It is not safe for you to stay here any more than it is for me."

I help Auguste pack what he feels is possible to take along and then realize his vast number of paintings stand patiently all round us. "What will you do with all your artwork, Auguste?"

"What can I do? They will belong to the Germans soon enough. Perhaps they will take pity and not destroy them."

"But this is your life's work!"

"Like my life, they too are fleeting. Besides, isn't it the duty of the next generation to create new art for their own generation?"

"I think many artists, both contemporary and from the past, would disagree with you, Auguste. I would think they'd prefer immortality to fleeting."

"Come, Nora, there will be days to paint once again."

I think to ask about the whereabouts of the portrait Auguste did of Ella and me and how nice it would be to see the two of us together again after so many years. But I decide the painting would only stir emotions long ago vaulted in my memories.

As we make our way south in Auguste's carriage toward the outskirts of the city, we encounter countless Parisian refugees pouring out of the city as though it were in flames. Entire families, including the elderly and children, travel away from what is certain to come.

"We move so slowly, Auguste."

"Trust me, Nora, this is much quicker than the railways."

Auguste knows the country well, and after a few days of travel, he calculates where we should break from the caravan of refugees and search for a secluded environ.

We, along with several dozen others, are received in the tiny village of Mar-sur-Alliers. Auguste explains how his ancestry dates back to the Nievre region.

"Traditional clockmakers," he explains, "all the way back to the seventeenth century."

The village elders, none too impressed with Auguste's heritage, appear to ruminate over the influx of refugees. Nevertheless, we're permitted to set up camp with the others in the woods nearby.

We have traveled a great distance today, but I find myself not the least bit tired. I am ready to help set up camp and provisions similar to Tolstoyan protocol. I am not so inclined to adhere to strict Tolstoyan doctrine under these circumstances and welcome the input of both Parisians and local villagers in establishing means of providing both security and order in our new home.

"This is a new change, Nora," says Auguste as he wanders about our new setting, his cane pointing at me. "You have acquired the gift of leadership?"

"I have acquired the gift to survive," I say, "even we lowly peasants of God need to provide for ourselves."

"We city-dwellers will be lucky to have you in our midst then. And we'll all need the mercy of God to survive."

In the evening, a fire is built and used to prepare several pots of vegetables and rice soup for nearly fifty people. It is well received after a long day's journey.

The following morning, there is an eagerness among the refugees to help cultivate the nearby fields. Even Auguste shows an interest in dirtying his hands with the good earth. Of course, he approaches such an endeavor the same way he does a new painting.

"You can't just rush in, Nora. It is useless to expect the plow to drop everything it is doing and rush into the job."

"So do you talk circles around your brushes as well?"

"But of course. The brush has been lazing about all night, and one mustn't expect it to jump up and attack the canvas. One must discuss the matter."

"Intelligently, no doubt."

"Yes, intelligently. But if that does not work, then you must maneuver around the brush, contemplating its position, suggesting to it that it is uncomfortable and that it should welcome the warmth of reclining in one's hand. And that is what I am about with the plow just now."

"Goodness, Auguste, aside from the oddness, it sounds like more work than would otherwise be required if you just took the plow in hand and began in earnest."

I solicit help from the nearby elderly farmers who know their crops and the season better than we new arrivals.

With the growing season nearly half gone, ground is quickly broke for a garden.

Auguste informs us of our isolation. "I have been told we are so remote that contact with the central government will be at a minimum."

"Provided said government remains intact, of course."

"Of course."

❦

*August 1915*

Thanks to the remoteness of our little village, we have survived a full year without being detected by friend or foe. We occasionally received word over the past several weeks that the front is closing in on us. Unfortunately, the German army is making gains into France.

The dirt road to the north lazily meanders through the thick trees. The leaves hang patiently in the air as the rumbling grows louder from round the bend. The noise has taken the place of the constant shelling that has kept me awake the past several nights. Most of the villagers and refugees are too afraid to make a decision. They pace about, back and forth, from one foot to the other, one foot suggesting they should hide in the woods, while the other foot says they should stay where they are and meet their fate.

A shopkeeper's wife, a middle-age woman from the Saint Germain District of Paris, is nearly hysterical, contemplating our fate aloud more so than anyone else. Her face bears much pain as she begs loudly to God for rescue. Someone tells her to shut up. She looks to where the voice came from and now appears ready to fight us all. Finally, she sits down on a tree trunk.

Teodor stands in front of me with his hands on his hips. I am standing along the roadside, holding Auguste's arm. He pats the back of my hand after feeling my trembling.

"I hope to be half as brave as you, Auguste," I say.

"It is easy for old men to be brave." He sighs while appearing resolute as he stares down the road toward the bend. They have less to live for."

"Are we less?" I ask.

He looks to me and Teodor as I smile. "Live for us, Auguste. You don't want me to be alone in your country, do you?"

Again he pats my hand but this time, I believe, to give me strength rather than comfort.

Now the rumbling changes to a grinding that is mechanical in tone. I can see the front of a tank as Auguste had earlier described them. There are soldiers on either side. The question remains whether or not they are French or German soldiers.

The soldiers' movements appear determined.

Teodor takes a step forward. I want to shout his name and tell him to get back, but the noise grows louder. He has become surly this past year and difficult to manage. Some nights, he runs with abandon through the countryside with other boys his age.

I imagine it is a way for him to find a place here, a Russian boy a long ways from home.

A man up ahead is jumping up and down, spinning and waving his arms in the air.

"They are French!" someone nearby shouts.

There is loud cheering. Now everyone is gathering along the road as if a parade were streaming through the village.

I feel relief and embrace Auguste. I notice that Teodor does not share in the excitement. I imagine him wanting to be a long way off, fighting beside his father.

Auguste returns from a combined village-military meeting and explains that the hierarchy has changed with the arrival of the French command. The village elders retain their positions, but the decisions regarding the distribution of food, shelter, and work detail is determined by the command. All current residents are to be interviewed and given work assignments.

I meet with an American captain named Browning who is also a physician.

"It is wonderful to speak with someone in English," I say, perhaps sounding a little too relieved.

He greets my smile with hesitation. I explain further that I have not been to America in fifteen years.

"That *is* a long time." I watch as he writes something down on a notepad.

"We had not heard America had entered the war."

"It hasn't. We're here for humanitarian reasons only."

I explain my background to the captain. It is decided that I should help as a nurse in the field hospital erected a mile from the village.

"But I have a son to tend to," I say.

"Thirteen, did you say?"

"Yes. And quite able for his age."

"In spite of his Russian descent, he should be allowed to attend school."

America will have to wait. There is much good that can be accomplished here.

*May 1916*

Having committed it to memory, I am drawing a scene of the devastation I saw today of a small town about five miles north of the base camp.

The Germans had retreated earlier, so it was finally safe for medical personnel to enter. We had quickly gathered, treated, and mobilized the injured and made our way back to the hospital. There were a number of homes still smoldering when we arrived. Someone pointed to a number of corpses lying on the road. I am certain two were of a grandfather and grandson leaving home, I imagined, and off to a day's toil in the field. There is a tin canister on its side between them and a blue-checkered cloth revealing the midday meal that would not be shared, all lying in the dirt. *This is war?* I now ask myself. *How is this honorable?*

Auguste looks over my shoulder, "Hmmm..." he begins, "I see you have improved your technique over the years. It is less about the mechanics now, no?"

"Your past advice has been taken well in hand, Auguste. I have come to give emotion to my drawings and paintings. Of course, it is through the suffering of humanity I feel the most emotion."

"I'm glad, Nora."

I am not.

*June 1918*

I have lost my son. He leaves me a note explaining that his place is in Russia and not here. I am overcome with worry now that I have spent the previous night wailing into my pillow.

I contact Captain Browning for assistance.

"I'm sorry, Nurse," he explains. "It is a civilian matter. And besides, I do not see how he can make his way from here all the way to the Eastern Front."

"He will make it—after all, he is his father's son—unless you will send out a patrol to try to catch him."

"You need to understand there are greater issues demanding the attentions of the military. I pity your situation, but you must appreciate the circumstances in which we find ourselves."

The lack of help I receive reminds me of the past. I am apt to believe the sole purpose of organs of authority is to intervene only when it is too late.

*August 1918*

I receive a letter six months old from my sister Ida, a welcome diversion under the circumstances.

*Dearest Nora,*

*I hope this letter finds you well and safely tucked away from the dangers of the war. We are all well here, and everyone sends their best.*

*The latest news is our little brother Teddy has become a father. Can you imagine that little man all grown up, married, and starting a family? It seems like only yesterday when he dumped a bucket of water over you from the top of the stable. Remember how you spent all day looking for him in the woods and how you pressed me to tell you where he was? I wanted to tell you he was in the water tower, but you were so angry I think it best I didn't. Anyway, he and Hannah had a daughter February $2^{nd}$. Her name is Norma. She is a lively child with much interest in everything around her. I think of you when I look into her face. Teddy will be busy working his own farm and raising crops and children.*

*In other news, we have become good little citizen-soldiers here, as we have signed on to President Hoover's Food Pledge. It started last April, when everyone was asked to have meat-less Monday and wheatless Wednesday. But now it has increased to seven meatless meals and seven wheatless meals and five both meatless and wheatless meals, leaving only two unrestricted meals every week. I hope you are seeing the benefits of our sacrifice. Mama tells me often of Papa's complaining about how it is possible for a farmer to have so much food in the ground but so little on his plate.*

*Do you remember the Wilson boys? Tobie and Jacob? You might run across them someday while you're in France. They shut down their mill and signed up last summer to help with setting up camps and roadways over there. Many other local boys have enlisted to fight in Europe.*

*Please write when you have the chance, and we all pray for this war to end soon. In the meantime, stay safe and sound.*

*Sincerely,*

*Your loving sister*

It is hard, but I am able to find the strength to accept the absence of Teodor. I lose myself in my nursing, and there is plenty of that to be had.

I have come across many casualties here at hospital from various walks of life. One such man, an American pilot from Minnesota, whose plane was severely damaged and who suffered a serious leg wound, told me of his account while attempting to destroy balloons, of all things, across enemy lines.

"It is the more proficient pilots that are tasked to do this very dangerous work."

"But, balloons?" I ask, "What is the object?"

"You see, they are used by the Hun to aim their artillery at our troops on the ground. So you can see that it's better they shoot at me, one pilot, than at many soldiers on the ground."

"Elmer, I'm sure your parents are quite proud of you."

"But they are so far away. I think a kiss from a very pretty Minnesota nurse would serve as consolation for the absence of family. Wouldn't you agree?"

"Kisses are for lovers and babies. And we're not lovers."

"But I used to be a baby. Won't you help me to remember what it is like to be kissed as a baby?"

After looking around the room, I quickly gave him a peck on the cheek.

"Ah, much obliged, Nurse Thorsen. You are most definitely a saint among the infirmed."

I can see on the wall clock that my shift is ending. "Time for you to rest." I forcefully tuck the covers up under his chin and bid him a good night. In my mind, the only benefit of the war is finding others from back home.

As I walk outside, I ponder the stars. It is a clear, cold night, and the calmness is interrupted by the faintest of explosions far off in the distance.

"G'evening, Nurse!"

I quickly spin round. "You startled me, Sergeant."

Sergeant Wentz, Captain Browning's assistant, steps from one foot to the other. His fair complexion does nothing to increase his short stature. He is the first real southerner I have met, and I find him distasteful. I have seen first-hand his disdain for Captain Browning. He is very respectful to his face, but I once witnessed his callousness behind his back.

"Hell! I'm twice the leader Browning is," I had heard him say to a group of enlisted men. "You stick with me, boys, and you'll not want for direction."

I know nothing of a soldier's life, but I suspect Sergeant Wentz is the type of leader who would take advantage of the situation, whether or not it benefited his men.

"I am available, ma'am, should you require an escort back to your quarters."

"That won't be necessary, Sergeant. But thank you." My pace is quick.

❧

*November 1918*

The line is breaking down. And so is Captain Browning's level of tolerance. Besides the endless stream of casualties, there appears to be an increase in self-inflicted wounds. And this, Captain Browning has no patience for. He can detect right away the signs. He explains them to me each time one is brought in on a stretcher. "This man before us has clearly taken his own dagger and driven it into his own thigh," the captain explains. Unfortunately, he has come dangerously close to his femoral artery.

"Don't these men know what they're fighting for?" he asks rhetorically as his spectacles flex up and down upon his nose, nostrils flaring. The shuffling of his mustache back and forth makes me bristle.

I continue to soak up the blood from the hemorrhaging. "There are different kinds of bravery, Captain."

"Yes, I know. There is the bravery found in the fearless and the bravery of the honorable."

"And there is the bravery of the man who wants to live another day," I say while raising my voice over the screams of the injured soldier, "in the hopes of being with those he loves."

"More suction here, Nurse Thorsen!" the captain shouts in return.

"I need help with holding the man," I protest.

"Wentz!" the captain snaps.

Suddenly, Sergeant Wentz steps into the tent. "Shouldn't we move out with the others, sir?" he pleads while the sound of distant mortars grows closer.

"How? I can't move this man until the bleeding stops. Come over here and help hold him still!"

The French corporal riles in pain, shouting, "*Arrêter la douleur, veuillez!*"

"Good God, man! Lie still! Nurse! More chloroform."

I hold the soldier's head firm to the stretcher and secure the inhaler to his face. While doing so, I am able to hear the lieutenant speak to the captain in no uncertain terms. "You are most certainly putting this nurse at risk, sir."

"Wentz!" the captain shouts. "I've known you long enough to realize you're only thinking of your own skin."

I see the contempt in the sergeant's eyes for both me and Captain Browning.

"That's better, Nurse," says the captain. "Once I secure this clamp, we will make a hasty retreat. Sergeant, fetch the corpsman."

The sergeant sticks his head out of the tent for only a moment and without so much as a word, ducks back inside.

"Ready, Sergeant?"

"Gone, sir."

"Are you sure?"

"Gone."

"Come then. Help me load this man into the truck."

I quickly begin to gather the equipment.

"Leave that," he orders. "We need to get out of here now."

The shelling has stopped. I can sense a strange quietness all around us as the captain and the sergeant load the injured soldier. As the sergeant shuts the back door of the truck, we all stop and listen. I stop breathing for the moment. The eeriness is amplified by ominous haze drifting from the battlefield and creeping all around us. It provides neither cover nor comfort. I think how contrary the setting to the security I had felt back at home in Minnesota on any foggy, rainy day.

"I'll drive," insists the captain.

Now we were making our way west over the muddy terrain, back to the British line.

We have traveled only a short distance when the vehicle becomes stuck.

I try to steady the injured soldier as the captain attempts to roll the ambulance back and forth in the mud.

After several attempts, the vehicle stops rocking. We are stuck, motionless and open to the elements.

I wait with the injured man in back while the men debate our situation.

Only a moment has passed when I hear the sergeant's strained voice. "Look! Who is that coming?"

And then I hear someone shout, "Halt! Halt!"

Now I hear the sergeant shouting, "Don't shoot! Don't shoot!" I see both the captain and the sergeant scrambling to exit the front of the ambulance.

I continue to administer to the injured man as the back door of the ambulance violently swings open.

I instantly conclude we have crossed paths with a lone soldier who must be separated from his unit.

Once the German soldier peers in the back of our ambulance, he grabs the French soldier by the boot and quickly pulls him out the door, dropping him like a sack of potatoes to the ground. He then begins to run him through with his bayonet. Mortified, I instinctively lurch toward the dying soldier, but the German aims his gun in my direction. The captain steps in between us and attempts to communicate with our captor.

*"Beruhigen Sie sich! Beruhigen Sie sich!"*

The German soldier points his rifle at the captain while ignoring his plea for calm. *"Bewegung, Arzt!"* He directs our movements with his rifle.

With the ambulance incapacitated, we're forced at gunpoint to begin walking back toward the direction of the battlefield. The haze is now replaced by a light mist. As we walk, the captain takes off his spectacles to wipe them with his kerchief and, while doing so, glances back in the direction of our captor.

I have never been this close to the actual front, where the men on both sides of the trenches lay dead. It is eerily disturbing to see so many lifeless corpses as far as the eye can see. The filth and the stench of death are overwhelming. At least men who lay dying on the operating table or in triage still have a fighting chance.

These poor souls, on the other hand, are lost to this world forever.

I start to wonder if today I will die.

Some time has passed when we finally climb a hill where the bark of several trees is clear of shrapnel and the grass mounds free from bloody soil. The desolation and death now lay behind us. The sky begins to clear as we near the top, at which point, we see three or four tents with a dozen or so men gathered about and mingling. This is the enemy's camp.

A few of the German soldiers come up to us and shake our hands as our captor directs us to enter one of the tents. They speak their native tongue, so we do not understand what they are saying. Our captor starts to rejoice as well, only with tears of exhaustion.

I am blinded by a number of lanterns staged around a body stretched out on a table.

A corporal approaches us and asks Captain Browning, "Are you a doctor?"

"Remember, Wentz. Name, rank, and serial number."

"Captain," I say, "I think they are in need of a doctor for the man on the table."

"If that is, in fact, the case, I say outrageous!"

Sergeant Wentz stands quietly in the corner of the tent appearing anything other than brave.

"Don't you feel you have a duty as a doctor to help, Captain?" He looks me straight in the eyes, but I cannot tell if he is angry or agreeable. Before the captain can respond, I am startled by the sound of my name.

"Nora?"

I instantly recognize the voice. The prone figure on the table is wearing the uniform of a German major, but it is the dark-brown handlebar mustache and goatee belonging to the chiseled face of my long-ago friend that stirs my memories.

"Tristan!"

"My," he stammers, "how you have become quite the lady."

"Are you in very much pain?"

"Yes. I need the skill of a good surgeon." He looks at the captain for assurance. "Is he such a surgeon, Nora?"

"And why should I aid and abet the enemy?" says the captain, indignant. "Why would I provide comfort to you?"

"Because it's all over."

"What is all over?" I ask, hoping against all hope.

"The war," he answers, clutching his left side.

"I don't believe it." The captain guffaws.

"Thank God," I say.

"It's true. I have the dispatch, if you can read German."

"I don't believe for a minute the allies have surrendered."

"On the contrary, sir; it is my side who has surrendered."

I am excited by the news as I take Tristan's hand in mine. "But your charges were rejoicing when we walked into camp."

"Win or lose, aren't all soldiers glad once the fighting has stopped?"

"If the war is over," the captain interrupts, "then I demand the right to return to my unit."

"If I could trouble you first to remove this piece of shrapnel lodged in my thigh, quite near my femoral artery. As you can see, the bleeding is under control, but I have had no one at my disposal brave enough to remove it."

"That's strange. I performed a similar operation earlier today. Unfortunately, it didn't take."

"That's a shame. But I'm sure it wasn't due to your proficiency as a medical doctor."

"No. It was a result of one of your men brutally murdering my patient."

Tristan appears dumbfounded.

"Of course he will operate," I respond. "And I'll be more than happy to assist."

"I don't have my equipment."

"All you need," answers Tristan, pointing, "is right over there. I too am a medical doctor."

I look at the captain, pleadingly.

"This is a friend of yours, Nurse?"

"Yes, from many years ago."

"I am doing this for you, Nora," he whispers. "It is hard enough under the circumstances."

"But, Captain, the war is over."

"Had we known that this morning, you might not have had to witness one of your friend's men murder a defenseless man."

"Let us hope his was the last life stolen by this war."

I ask Tristan to be quiet and rest while I nurse his wound. But he is anxious to talk. I too am curious about the years dividing our last encounter.

"So tell me, Nora, where has your life taken you? Do you have a family?"

"I have a sixteen-year-old son who has gone missing behind enemy lines. I fear he has either been captured or killed by the Germans. I should wonder how it is I can stand to talk to you, Tristan." His expression is serious. His disposition hasn't changed in all these years. I give him a smile.

"Ah, I see. I remember now how much you liked to tease me. But perhaps I can be of service in locating your son."

I know Tristan is merely being kind and that the odds are quite slim in locating Teodor under the current chaos that makes up the world around me; nonetheless, I am grateful for the suggestion. "That would be wonderful. Please do what you can."

"Certainly. I will send word down the line in search of a lost sixteen-year old whose mother is worried sick. But what else have you been doing all these years?"

"I have spent many years in southern Russia, teaching and painting."

"You have been with the French painter all these years?"

"Heavens, no. We parted company many years ago, but we were reunited when this silly war broke out."

I tell him of my many years living a simple life on Yasnaya Polyana. I don't expect Tristan to praise my decision, but neither am I ready to hear him denounce Tolstoy.

Tristan adjusts the bandage on his thigh as he begins to speak. "I may be on the wrong side, but I believe it is those like Tolstoy who make wars inevitable."

"I couldn't disagree more. Tolstoy was a proponent of non-violence."

"And a proponent of non-resistance, which, in and of itself, is a form of resistance."

"You'll have to elaborate someday, but now I wish you would rest."

"Nora, I could tell you of things I have seen and learned over the years. I have witnessed the cruelty of suffering at the hands of man and of nature. When you see a human being dying and you are helpless to stop it, you find the answers to the mysteries of life through knowledge rather than through religious faith."

"I shouldn't wish to debate you on that point just now. I'd rather you rest." I rise to walk away.

"Nora." I turn around once again to discourage Tristan from saying another word, but I can see in his eyes how important it is for him to speak. "Do you remember the last time we spoke in New York?"

"Yes, of course. I was very angry at the time. I said things I didn't mean."

"I don't remember those things you didn't mean, but I know you meant it when you said you're not like Ella, how you had no interest in settling down and marrying."

"I'm sorry I hurt you, Tristan."

"I may have been hurt, but I realized how different you were from other women. And now you should realize how different you are this day because of your choices, because of your free will."

"Whatever choices I've made, I feel blessed."

"Please, Nora, hear me out. I suspect you will be leaving first thing in the morning, and I just want to ask you to think about how your choices were made by you and no one or anything else."

As I stand there staring into Tristan's eyes, I can't help but imagine how life had hardened his soul. I begin to walk away again, wishing the two of us could return to Central Park and our youth, if only to reconsider the future with today's perspective.

*December 1918*
At the base camp, there are soldiers wandering round carefree and looking confident, as surely the future will be much brighter now that hostilities have come to an end.

I enjoy the mile walk into the village to see Auguste. He will no doubt have missed me as much as I have missed him. It is a funny surprise for me to learn how much I do love him.

"Have you been to your parents' homeland, Nora?"

"No. But I've always wanted to go there."

"You should go someday. Go to Oslo. Find the great works from your true countrymen. Munch. Tidemand."

"I am comfortable in the fact that I have known France's greatest artist."

"So kind of you." He smiles as his eyes begin to glaze over. "What a terrible way to die," he laments. "And you, Nora, are my only regret."

"I'm so sorry, Auguste," I begin to plead as I cool his forehead with the damp cloth. "I wanted so much to love you the way you wished me to."

"None of that. My regret lies only in having not captured your likeness in the most heavenly of poses. You were the new style of painting that never was. The movement that budged not an inch. The exhibit that only heaven will show."

"I wish I could have been more to you. At least a proper and willing poser."

"That you ever existed is the most rewarding feeling of all."

"I think I could pose for you now, Auguste, any way you would allow me. Just please get better." I kiss his cheek.

"I don't think there is such a thing as 'better' for an aging and dying man."

He begins to strain for air. He gasps and then takes long deep breaths. I think to leave him to rest and start to rise from the bed, but he reaches for my arm.

"Nora," he asks, as though something has just occurred to him, "do you still pray to your god in heaven?"

"But of course, Auguste." My hand finds his frail shoulder. "Particularly now, as it is His birthday tomorrow."

"Maybe … maybe you could pray to him for me."

"Or maybe you could do it yourself. He's right here." I place my hand over his heart. "He's always been here, my dear Auguste."

He smiles and stares up at the ceiling with tear-filled eyes, and whispers, "Thank you, dearest Nora."

❧

"I don't understand."

"I'm sorry, Nurse, but I can't be more clear than to repeat that you are being called before the tribunal on charges of fraternizing with the enemy."

"Who has brought these charges against me?" Shocked, I have already forgotten the man's name who is serving me a summons.

"Captain Browning."

I am now dumbfounded. I have always believed Captain Browning and I had been on the best of terms in spite of our contrary opinions regarding the war.

"I should like to speak with him."

"Out of the question."

"Why not?"

"He is away from camp. And even if he were here, it would be ill-advised for you to speak directly to your accuser."

"Will I not be allowed to confront my accuser?"

"I believe the summons should answer any further questions."

❧

I find myself feeling quite weak the day of the hearing, but I want desperately to exonerate myself of Captain Browning's accusation, so I prepare myself best I can and proceed to the office of the tribunal.

I sit down next to my counsel, a Captain Holmsted, whom I find quite sympathetic to my position and whom I feel a kinship to, as both of us grew up in the Midwest.

"Nora," he begins, "you do not look at all well this morning. Given the circumstances, I can understand some sign of anxiety…"

"I am not well," I interrupt him. "I fear I have contracted the flu."

The captain appears to flinch upon hearing this. "My apologies, Nora, but don't you think I should seek a postponement of the hearing until you are feeling better?"

"No!" I am resolute. "I need to get this behind me immediately."

During the proceedings, Sergeant Wentz is called to testify against me. His demeanor is that of his usual overconfidence. I feel his testimony is sketchy at best and suggest to Captain Holmsted that he need not cross-examine Wentz, as I feel we need to get to the heart of the matter by way of Captain Browning. He agrees but suggests to me that Wentz's character could be called into question, creating a possible advantage to my case. He asks that I consider this until after the prosecutor's direct exam.

My head begins to throb more than before, and my neck has a stiffness confirming my self-diagnosis that I have indeed contracted the flu.

After Sergeant Wentz is sworn to tell the truth before God and the court, the prosecution comes directly to the point. "Sergeant Wentz, on the eleventh of November, 1918, did you, in fact, witness the defendant engaging the enemy in a manner inconsistent with United States Army regulations?"

"Yes, sir."

"Sergeant Wentz, please describe in your own words the circumstances leading up to this offense."

"Well, we had been captured by a German soldier while attempting to return to base and were forced to march across no man's land and into enemy territory. There, we were met by more German soldiers."

The sergeant continues with his testimony, explaining in detail the encounter with Tristan and Captain Browning's operation.

"Sergeant Wentz, if you could describe the defendant's demeanor toward this officer?"

"Well, sir, it was clear to me and the captain that Nurse Thorsen knew the German officer."

"Objection," says Captain Holmsted. "The witness is attempting to speculate as to what Captain Browning knew during the incident."

"Sustained. Sergeant Wentz," says the head judge, "please speak to your own knowledge regarding the events of the case in question."

"Yes, sir."

The prosecution continues. "Sergeant Wentz, please describe the conduct of the defendant while she was engaged with the enemy officer."

"Well, sir, right off, she shared pleasantries with the enemy officer that suggested to me they had been long acquainted."

"Such as?"

"Later that evening, sir, we were sitting around the fire, and I overheard the defendant and the enemy officer discussing at length things of a personal nature."

"Such as?"

"How they had been intimate during the war."

Hearing this lie, I immediately feel a rush of anger running counter to my feeling of malaise. And just as I am about to agree with Captain Holmsted how necessary it is to cross-examine Wentz, I begin to slowly tilt to one side of my chair.

When I awake, Captain Holmsted is standing over me, patting the back of my hand while requesting a glass of water.

⁂

*January 1919*

I have, indeed come down with the same malady that took the life of Auguste. I am isolated from the other patients. I can feel my strength dwindling each day.

Something deep from my past beckons me, something borne of the fear of death and the lack of family around me. I now wish to be back in the comfort of the house I grew up in, to be ministered by my mother, to be blessed by the pastor of my country church.

A nurse appears before me. She places a cool, damp cloth on my forehead. Before she steps away, I ask her to please summon the chaplain. She returns to inform me that the base hospital chaplain is of the Catholic faith and asks if that is all right. I have nothing against Catholics but wonder if it would be possible to locate a Lutheran chaplain.

I am relieved to learn a Lutheran chaplain is en route from a nearby military camp.

The following afternoon, during our meeting, the chaplain asks if I would like to receive the holy sacrament. Again feeling an overwhelming need to travel back to my past, I gladly accept.

"If only you could give me Holy Communion in the Norwegian language."

"That I can. And I will."

"Really? Are you Norwegian, Chaplain."

"Yes. I am a Norwegian from Wisconsin."

"This is a Christmas miracle."

"It's already the new year, but *Glaedelig Jul* just the same, Nora!"

"Thank you! *Glaedelig Jul* to you as well. It's been so long since I've heard *Merry Christmas* spoken to me in Norwegian."

"How long have you been away from home?"

"Nearly twenty years now."

"That *is* a long time. Haven't you missed seeing your family all those years?"

"There have been many letters, but they don't replace being there long side everyone at the dinner table, eating big meals and speaking of the changes in our lives." I stop to take a deep breath.

"Nora, please stay calm. I promised your nurses I would keep you relaxed. We mustn't let them think I am a man who breaks his promises."

I smile as my memories rush forth. "I was on my way to be with them just before this silly war began. And now that I find myself lying here dying, I'm a little ashamed to admit I'm homesick for them at this time of year."

The chaplain leans in and whispers, "There is home, and then there is *home*."

"Yes. I am not afraid to die. I know I don't have much time. If you could please tell my folks that I believe that Jesus died for me and he will welcome me into heaven."

The chaplain visits me over the next several days. He provides devotional readings until I am to the point where I cannot understand him. My mind begins to wander, and sleepiness increases as the world grows dark around me.

*What if you died? I hear a voice, quiet, reserved, speaking, "Nora is a fine and loving daughter. She was very dependable on the farm, but both her mother and I knew she had a higher calling. We are both very proud to learn she has served well in the army. Please, Doctor, do whatever you can to help her to return to this world."*

*What if you died? I see a little girl running away from me. I cannot see her face, but I know she is running because she is sad. I made her unhappy. I made her cry. I am clutching an old, hand-me-down doll. To not share, to not be a gracious host, now to be filled with shame. I will make Ella my friend for life.*

*What if you died? I lie facedown on the cool grass, tears clouding my vision as I finally regain my breath. I curse the tree while waiting for someone to run over and lift me from the ground, but no one comes. No one has witnessed my foolishness. I am ready to learn that the world is no place to be alone.*

*What if you died? I am protective of Ella, more so than I am of my young brothers and sisters. I see Ella as more than a sibling. She is a kindred spirit. I deflect the taunting by the local boys. Ella wonders if it is something we bring on ourselves. I tell her it's this place and its backwardness.*

*We need to get out of here someday, run far away, and never look back. Her look is filled with doubt.*

*Someone dies. I see the doubt etched in Ella's face staring up at me. She bobs up and down in the water; her hair floats about her head. Now I realize I too have died, over and over.*

*Jesus died for me. I see an empty crucifix and think of Christ. I think about my own place on that cross, not for saving the world but more so as one of the criminals that died beside Jesus. I wait, longingly, for him to tell me how I will be in paradise with him today. I wait and wait.*

*April 1919*

I hear the rattling of medical equipment below the din of my own accelerating breathing. I feel the tears streaming down and around my ears as I lie staring up at the dim light above me. I try to stir but feel quite weak. I start to cry, feeling in a state between reality and fiction.

"There, there." I hear a voice. "You're just fine, Nora. Lie still while I fetch the doctor."

I lie here pondering the moonlight shining through the opening to the large tent. It feels like I am not quite out of the darkness. I reflect on my last thoughts before waking, trying to draw a correlation between them and what I am now perceiving.

"Welcome back, Nora." I look up to see the face of Captain Browning.

I feel apprehensive but manage to ask, "Where am I?" while imagining I must be in a military prison hospital.

"Don't you recognize the old Number Sixty-Eight with its white canvas, white bed sheets, and white faces, all so different from the other base camp hospitals?"

"I guess I do, at that," I say with a half smile. "What has happened to me?"

"I don't want to give you a start, so maybe you should continue to rest."

"Rest? How? I don't know if I'm coming or going. How can I rest?"

"Very well, Nora. You had the flu for a number of days, and then you fell into a coma."

"For how long?"

"Nearly three months. You are the last of our patients."

"I see." I think how much must have happened in the three months I was not able to make my way back to Yasnaya Polyana.

"But please rest for now, Nora," Captain Browning pleads. "You have a long recovery ahead of you, and you are too weak to exert so much energy in conversation."

I nod. Captain Browning begins to walk away. "But, Captain," I ask, "what of my court-martial?"

"No need to worry about that matter, Nora. Water under the bridge. Let's just say that Wentz has been summarily dealt with for his actions, least of which was his forging of my name to official documents. I shouldn't, if I were you, give him a second thought."

I am too relieved to worry about the reasons behind Sergeant Wentz's ill intentions toward me and do just as the doctor prescribed.

I am feeling much better as I rest on the stone wall that borders between the fields of the hospital camp and the local farmer to the south. The little village of Mars-sur-Allier lies to the west as the high sun watches over it from above. I imagine the new life its people are experiencing, one of peace and tranquility. I imagine the gardens freshly planted, the vineyards long absent of harvest, and how the world looks so much brighter in the aftermath of so much chaos.

"Good afternoon, Nora." I turn to see Captain Browning approach. His hat is pulled down lower than usual to help deflect the bright sun. "Any more brilliant, and that field filled with flecks of Spanish Brooms will blind us all."

"I'm feeling so much better, Captain."

"Yes, you've come along quite nicely. The Bourgogne air has done wonders for your well-being."

"I think I'm well enough to travel into the village this afternoon. I have a friend I'd like to see."

Captain Browning appears perplexed but acquiesces. "I should like to drive you there. I don't think it wise of you to walk, even though it is only a mile or so down the road."

I smile and nod. "Captain, do you think this country will ever be the same?"

"Who can say?" he begins. "A war can leave such a debilitating mark on the land and its people." He turns away in reflection. "Think of our own country's big war. If you look closely enough, Nora, you can still see the scars that exist where brother killed brother." His words seem to catch sail in the breeze moving across the field.

As we pass the old mill near the river and stop at the nearby cemetery, I think of the little river running near my parents' homestead and the small church and cemetery just down the road, tucked away behind the trees, and how the wind rushing through their fullness sounded like the waves from an ocean.

"I'll wait here, Nora," says the captain.

I walk over to Auguste's grave. The freshness of the mound reminds me just how short a time it has been since his passing. I had petitioned the village to allow him to be buried in their little cemetery, explaining his passion for art and how his greatest works were those of the land and its people. They were honored. It seemed little enough for a man who loved his country above all else.

"Dear Auguste, I hope you have found peace here. I know it is a long way from your beloved Paris, and I hope you will forgive me, as I too am going a long way from here. God bless you, Auguste."

# A Foolish Son

A wise son brings joy to his father, but a foolish son grief to his mother.

Proverbs 10:1

*June 1919*

"I think it ill-advised, Nora," repeats Captain Browning, "for you to travel through this war-torn continent. There is, no doubt, a shortage of food and plenty of lawlessness."

"Captain," I again explain, "please try and understand that I am compelled to return to Yasnaya Polyana in search of my son for those very reasons."

"Nora," Captain Browning continues, "I would appreciate your permission to allow me to accompany you to the Ukrainian border, where you intend to meet this artist friend you spoke of earlier."

"But you have your own life to live. I can't burden you with mine."

"Nonsense. I have already accepted an assignment with the American Relief Administration in Moscow. Russia is now a country on the precipice of chaos, and it will require a grand effort to avoid a complete breakdown of order."

"But Yasnaya Polyana is so far from Moscow. It would be far too great a journey out of your way."

"I will make no bones about my feelings toward you." He stands stiffly and stares just over my head. "I have grown fond of you during our service together, and I am concerned about your safety."

I both appreciate and understand the advantages of having Captain Browning escort me through territories that were once filled with peace but now might, in fact, be considered hostile. I do not make the captain wait long for his answer.

Captain Browning possesses papers providing us freedom of movement through various checkpoints across many countries. There are some areas where this is a simple matter. The inspections are orderly and reserved. But in other areas, we're met with hostility. Hungary provides a close call as the captain and I are interrogated by men claiming to represent the new government.

"If you are not common bandits, then would you kindly provide identification?" requests the captain.

"Of course, American," said the leader, a man whose bitterness is as visible as the sweat stain of his cap. "Allow me to wire the central government in Budapest. They no doubt are fully abreast of your movements."

"And may I ask how long that will take?"

"It could be days, since the infrastructure of the country is in dire condition as a result of allied aggression."

"That's absurd. There were never any allied forces that penetrated this far into Hungary."

"Perhaps not physically, but the scars are more subtle and deep. I would advise you to cooperate, as this town is not filled with praise for the allies in spite of the war's outcome."

We are detained in the small town of Paks, located about fifty miles south of Budapest. We're kept under house-arrest in a bombed-out jailhouse, and though our accommodations are less than satisfactory, it is certain the captain and I are much better off than many of the town's citizens.

Captain Browning does his best to keep my spirits up. "You'll see, Nora. We'll be on our way in no time. This is merely red tape we must cut through if we're to make any progress."

"Is there no other way we can go?"

"Afraid not, unless you are willing to entertain the notion of climbing through the mountains."

"It feels as though the war continues here."

"In some parts, I'm sure it does continue. There are many factions vying for control all across Hungary. Perhaps this is the case in many other countries across Europe who had the misfortune of being swept up in the kaiser's aggressions."

Peering through the barred window, I can see many locals wandering under the overcast sky. There is an eerie feeling as I watch people rummaging through destroyed buildings and overturned wagons. I imagine if these people are unable to find sustenance, then perhaps we would need to go hungry as well.

Our guard leaves us in the darkness.

"We might as well make the best of it, Nora," he says.

Our cell has only a wooden chair and a pallet made up of three planks. The captain offers me the pallet to sleep on. Without the lamp, the cell is nearly pitch dark, aside from the light from the quarter moon.

I am able to doze off, but then I begin to hear stirring. I call out to the captain, whose hunched-over silhouette is visible against the wall.

"Sorry to wake you, Nora, but I'm afraid we have a rat problem."

"Maybe you could catch it by the tail and let it loose out through the bars of the window."

"What I mean is that we have a rat problem involving many rats."

I feel I am immune to the fear of many things. The home I grew up in had many mice over the years. Even the barn was known to have a colony of bats every summer. But this business about rats I find unnerving.

"What can we do?"

"Guard!" The captain is determined in his tone. "Guard!"

The guard appears from the other room, his drowsiness accentuating his irritation.

"We need a light in our cell to keep away the rats."

"Stupid fool!" he shouts. "If you do not bother the rats, they will not bother you."

"Outrageous!" The captain is not through with the guard, but the guard is through with us, as he is walking back to the other room. "At least provide better accommodations for the lady!"

"You will be wise to keep quiet. You do not want to draw attention to yourselves in this town."

"How do you like that?" It is the captain's tone that keeps me from unraveling. It is desperate yet lighthearted.

"I'm so sorry I've brought you to this place."

"Not your fault, Nora. It's of my own doing. And in the end, I'm glad to have come to keep track of all the trouble you'll be getting yourself in."

Again, though it is dark and we are under siege, I can hear the humor in his voice.

The captain makes the best of our situation, spending most of the night seated on the floor at the side of the pallet, sliding the chair back and forth whenever he feels an advancement of rats. I offer to trade places with him so that he might rest awhile.

"I'm fine, Nora. Besides, I don't think I could sleep knowing you were awake taking care of this business."

"I can hardly sleep myself, for the same reason."

"You should try to rest."

"Perhaps you could talk to me so that I might eventually fall asleep."

"I can't think of anything to say, I'm afraid."

"Nonsense. Tell me about yourself. I realize now I don't really know that much about you."

"Rotten vermin!" He slides the chair back and forth across the floor like a prone pendulum, and while doing so, he speaks of a personal life I had not imagined, the loss of both mother and father when he was only eight years old, ten years in a boys' home in Saint Paul, and a medical degree complimented by a Saint Olaf University education.

"How did you come to lose your parents, Doctor?"

"In a fire, the most wicked of fires ever known to man. You've no doubt heard of the Great Fire of 1894?"

"Of course. The fire in the eastern Minnesota town of Hinckley. And you were only eight?"

"Yes."

"I imagine this life-changing event had something to do with your becoming a doctor?"

"Very perceptive. And a rather personal story."

"I'm sorry."

"No. That's all right. I feel as though I can share it with you, as we both have experienced loss in our lives. I will never forget the loss of my parents. We had boarded a train from Hinckley, heading north out of town in hopes of escaping the fire. I remember the train cars were very crowded—so crowded, there were many people on the roof of the cars, including my parents and me. As the train sped down the tracks, we could see the smoke and flames on either side of the train. And the heat was very intense and would come in waves. I remember how afraid I was and how tightly my mother held me.

"The next thing I know, I am being handed across from the rooftop of the car to the one in front of us. The last words I hear are of my mother's voice, telling me to let go of her. And I wouldn't have, but a man on the other car pulled me swiftly from my mother's grasp. As I looked back, I could see flames jumping all around the car my parents were riding atop. And then suddenly the car begins to grow smaller and smaller. Someone had disconnected it from the train. I still vividly recall the frantic scene of people jumping off and out of that car, some of the people running up the tracks only to be lost in the thick, dark smoke."

"But you were saved."

"Barely. As we traveled along, the flames kept pace with our train. At one point, when all seemed to be lost, the entire train began to slow, and people jumped from it and ran toward a nearby lake. Many were saved, but many perished."

"So that is why you chose to become a doctor."

"Yes. But what drew you to nurse's training so many years ago?"

"A tiresome tale I think I should like to save for another time, if you don't mind."

The captain stops sliding the chair around the room, and silence fills the cell. Just as I am about to speak, he says, "It should come as no surprise to you, Nora, that many consider you a very saintly woman because of your efforts not only as a nurse, but also as a settlement organizer in Mar-sur-Alliers."

"I appreciate hearing that, but I think it best to leave sainthood to those in heaven. I have not led a saintly life, I can assure you."

"I have no doubt your sins pale in comparison to those committed and witnessed by God during this horrible war."

I feign sleepiness only to avoid the topic but spend a restless night imagining the subtle differences between deliberate cruelty and deliberate selfishness.

⁂

I am woken by clanging against the cell bars. The captain is quick to his feet. "What are you doing?" he whispers harshly. "Can't you see this woman is resting?"

"You would rather sleep all day than be on your way?"

"It is about time." The captain turns to face me as I rub my tired eyes. "Nora. Evidently, we're free to go."

Then he turns back to the guard. "You've received a communiqué, I assume?"

"No communiqué. The commander tells me to let you out so that we are rid of you." The guard lets open the door.

As we walk out, the captain mumbles to me how he'd like to give the commander a piece of his mind, but I imagine he thinks it best to move on as quickly as possible.

The train is not expected for several days, so we continue our journey on foot.

We're able to find both hospitable and generous peasant folk along our travels. These people are either less concerned with or oblivious to the tragedies befalling the nation over the past four years and, instead, make allowances for weary travelers.

Two days after our release, we reach Budapest and embark on a transcontinental train heading for Kiev.

Cassandra meets me at the train station. We share a tight embrace. I introduce her to my escort, Captain Browning. She gives him a suspicious nod.

"It is wonderful to see you again, Nora, after so many years. You've changed."

"I think we both have, Cassandra."

"Yes. That is true." I love seeing her broad smile after so many years, though her eyes appear to be filled with caution. "We should make haste now that you have passed through immigrations. I would have thought your lack of a Russian accent would have given you trouble."

"My passport indicates that I'm a Russian. It seemed to be enough."

"It's a different country, Nora. There is civil war to the north, and no one is above suspicion. We have a new leader."

"Yes. I heard about this Lenin taking the place of the tsar."

"He is no tsar. That is most definite. I should tell you right off, Nora, that my resources are quite limited."

"What do you mean?"

"My family's property has been confiscated by the new Soviet government and is now the property of the people."

Outwardly, I sympathize with Cassandra's plight, but inwardly, I am pleased to hear this news. "It sounds to me as though the people have taken on the tenets of Tolstoy. Is everyone Tolstoyan now?"

"Hardly, my dear." She laughs and then searches the nearby crowd with a look of extreme caution. "Right now, it is best to keep quiet about such things."

"What are your immediate plans?" asks the captain.

I look to Cassandra for direction. "We're traveling east through the country. We must hurry if we are to make the train."

I can see the captain is disheartened by this news, as am I. I wish not to end our relationship so abruptly. "Thank you, Captain, for your assistance along these many miles."

He looks at Cassandra, wearily, and expresses his sadness. "I think we shall meet again someday, Nora. Perhaps back in America. You must promise to write me someday and let me know how things turn out for you."

"By all means." The captain is surprised when I reach to embrace him and whisper, "Thank you for saving my life."

⁂

*July 1919*
Cassandra and I make our way across Ukraine by train. There are many checkpoints at which every passenger needs to provide proof of identity. Not only does it become overbearing, but I begin to feel a sense of confinement, as though the train continues in a circle only to stop at the same spot each time.

"Cassandra, is it me, or does it feel as though we're moving about the country as though it were a wide open prison?"

"Not so loud, Nora. There are ears everywhere."

At a checkpoint east of Poltava, we see a man running away from the train and hear shots fired as the police pursue him.

I look at Cassandra but say nothing.

When we arrive in Charkiv, we search the city for accommodations and find a quaint and affordable boardinghouse near the center of the city. Even in this place, there is an air of fear of the unknown. The manager glances several times at the entrance as though he is expecting a great rush of some sort while a man sits with his back against the lobby wall, peering above his newspaper.

Once comfortably in our room, I begin to question what is going on all around us.

"As I said, Nora, my family's property was confiscated. My parents were arrested and sent to God knows where. I can't even find out, for fear I too will be arrested."

She hands me her papers. When I look at them, I see that the name does not match the face.

"Why are you traveling under an assumed name, Cassandra?"

"Don't you understand, Nora? I am part of the aristocracy that this Lenin is trying to eradicate."

I now feel as though my life is suddenly in jeopardy. I want to trust Cassandra but need to know that we're not somehow on the wrong side of the law.

"How can I be sure that we will be able to get back to Yasnaya Polyana so that I can be with my son?"

"I can only offer the security of someone who is a member of the underground movement."

"What is that?"

"It is part of the new war being waged within the Soviet Republic." Cassandra can see that I do not understand. "Nora, the country is in a civil war."

"But the war is over. Who is fighting whom?"

"Imagine the loyalists of the tsar, the wealthy, the military elites. They are waging a war against the new government, the Reds."

"The Reds, are they not bringing about positive change? You mentioned before that all property belongs to the people. Whose idea is that?"

"That is indeed Lenin's directive, but it is not based on a moral precept but rather by the use of godless force."

Suddenly, I feel sick to my stomach. I never imagined that so many people could be influenced by the beliefs of men rather than the teachings of God. I begin to wonder just where my son will fall into the scheme of things. Whom is he fighting for?

*August 1919*
There is an unkempt quietness about the estate's appearance. The past five weeks since our arrival have shown minimal activity. Where there should be active harvesting, there is only wild growth and stillness.

We hole up in the little house where I gave birth to my only living child. We're waiting for an opportunity to make our way north. Unfortunately, we have no idea how that opportunity may present itself. I conclude that it will be based mainly on a sense of semi-security. Cassandra tells me that maybe when we hear someone laughing, not so much out of fear or insanity but rather from a dose of true, healthy laughter, then maybe it will be time to go. But it is hard to look so far ahead and expect that the day will come when there is a sense of normality in the world.

The master's youngest daughter, Alexandra, is willing to meet with Cassandra and me. She appears to be formerly well fed, but her charcoal-colored dress now fits loosely. Her hair is up, revealing her entire face, which is somewhat sad and almost masculine in appearance. She too, like Cassandra, has remained unmarried all these years. I imagine these two opposites to be of the same kind, cautious of strangers yet quite willing to help in any way possible.

"Thank you for seeing us," I begin.

"Not at all. It is a welcome change from arguing with either bureaucrats or the Tolstoyans."

"Do the walls have ears?" asks Cassandra.

"I can only speak for this very room, though I do think most of the government charges are simpletons and therefore incapable of espionage."

"Regarding the Tolstoyans," I now ask, "surely you too are one?"

"I am referring to those who would rather sit idle while others do all the work. The majority of these so-called Tolstoyans are unnatural in their beliefs. I have lost all patience for them."

"What would your father think of your attitude toward his disciples?" asks Cassandra with a note of disdain.

"As I say, the majority are ill-mannered idlers and hardly worthy of being referred to as my father's followers. They claim to abide by his tenets, but they go about it distastefully. I have suggested schooling for their children and cultivation through art—things my father would very much approve of—and these idlers turn their noses up and suggest that it is ungodly. But enough about them. What can I do for you ladies?"

We explain our circumstances and plead for her assistance in any way.

"We have lost a great deal," she begins to explain. "I returned from the war to find our home ransacked. Everything gone. All that remained were my two white huskies I had raised as pups."

I begin to explain that I am in search of my son. "He has been lost to me nearly a year and a half."

Alexandra's tone accentuates her indifference. "Many have lost loved ones. It is the nature of war."

"Our families have a long history," said Cassandra. "Surely that counts for something."

"That depends. I suspect you are part of the 'save the monarch' movement perpetrated by the Whites, the tsar's officers and aristocratic friends."

"Would it not be more preferable than the current situation in which the country finds itself?" Cassandra asks without admitting to anything subversive.

"No. The time for tsars and the church has past. They had their chances and failed miserably."

"I should agree with you," I interject, realizing my new task of maintaining peace between these two strong-willed individualists, "but the current situation appears to have reduced the relevancy of individualism far below that of the collective."

"That observation is quite obvious. And this I know from personal experience. Everything that belonged to my family has been nationalized. It is as though I have become a stranger to everything I've known all my life."

"Yes," exclaims Cassandra. "You and I are one in the same."

"I doubt that very much. You are aching from your loss like a child deprived of a toy, while I, on the other hand, am at the same time both relieved and saddened. Not because I am now equal to everyone else, but because those things that were once sentimental to me have been lost in the wave of extreme and impersonal change."

Before Cassandra can respond to Alexandra's slight, I ask, "What can I do? I must find my son."

"Everyone has lost something as a result of the revolution. I have never been a mother, as I was committed to being with my father until his last days, but I know what it is to have lost someone. For me, it is very acute, as I was the one who closed his eyes after his last breath."

"Thank you for understanding my plight, but what can I do if not search for my son? Do you think it is so easy for a mother to forget about her own son?"

"In some ways, it is better that you forget and move on with your life. Russia is vast, and further travel is out of the question, as your papers are invalid and your friend's are forged. Nor can I allow you to stay on here and jeopardize the entire estate."

"You speak, Countess, of things we cannot do, but will you not help us in any way?" Cassandra's voice is filled with contempt.

"Please do not refer to me as Countess. Those days are gone, and I never prescribed to that title, even then."

"Again, won't you help us?" I plead.

"My suggestion to you is that you should make your way north to the settlements of the Dukhobors. From there, you might be able to make your way out of the country, perhaps to Finland. They are making great efforts to relocate many of their followers to Canada."

"But how can we get there from here?" I am still not entirely convinced that I should give up the search for Teodor, but I begin to consider the possibility of never seeing him again. "As you say, our papers are suspect, and we have little resources."

Alexandra pauses for some time, her face etched with contemplation. Finally, she speaks. "I leave for Moscow later this week. I may be able to transport the two of you that far without consequence."

"We would be very grateful."

As Cassandra and I walk from the Tolstoy residence, I can sense she is eager to say something.

"I don't understand, Nora."

"What do you mean?"

"You have given up finding Teodor so quickly."

"Not at all. It may appear underhanded, but I think Alexandra will come round and help me find him through her contacts. And Moscow will be a good place to make inquiries."

"You are very optimistic. I find her to be quite cold and indifferent. It will be difficult to trust her. But I am glad we're off to Moscow. I too have contacts, as you well know."

I begin to imagine my relationship with Cassandra will only lead to trouble.

❧

Alexandra's Moscow apartment is both small and sparse, which, I am certain, is due to her father's influence rather than the conditions placed on all Russians, including those former members of the aristocracy. I am moved by her generosity, which she has taken upon herself and with the possibility of great risk.

Alexandra stokes with kindling and lights the little samovar in the corner. "I will make us tea," she announces.

"That would be nice," I say. "Your home away from home is both cozy and humble."

"And once I am able to start a fire in my 'Lilliputian,' we will feel some warmth."

The stove is indeed small, and I do not hold out much hope that it will warm the three rooms that make up the little apartment.

*September 1919*

On occasion, Alexandra entertains an array of guests, most of which are old associates or disciples of her late father. She allows Cassandra to have people over for private meetings. While Cassandra conducts a meeting in the apartment, both Alexandra and I step out into the hallway. We sit on the steps looking down to the door by the street. I wrap my shawl around myself tightly, as there is a draft coming in from somewhere. She smokes a cigarette, inhaling deeply. She explains how it is a calming habit she picked up while serving in the war.

"My father would be very disappointed to see me puffing like a train."

I smile as she blows a ring of smoke in the air. "It is gracious of you to allow Cassandra's friends to meet in your apartment."

"They are good people who, like me, have lost everything. But they are very political, and I find such things to be very trying on my patience."

"I am the same. I think the politics of a matter tend to convolute the intent of the matter itself. Perhaps I see things too black or white."

"Politics will, indeed, mix those two colors beyond recognition."

I smile at her round face. "We have things in common. We are both apolitical. We served as nurses in the war. We both long for the meaning of God."

"God, war, and politics. If we have the same ideas about all three, then we must be soul sisters." Now she smiles at me. "Tell me, Nora, about your upbringing?"

"My childhood pales in comparison to one such as yours."

"I doubt that very much. If you grew up in a large family, always longing for the love of your parents, then I suspect we are again similar."

"That sounds about right, although I have been away from home these past twenty years, so it is my fault if my parents have forgotten that I still exist."

"You may be lucky. I have had the company of parents all my life, and it has been a strain, keeping them from warring."

"Surely yours was a happy home, was it not?"

"You probably imagine the wealth and fame of my father as a means to happiness."

"I certainly do not. I have read many of your father's works, and I agree that the only way to happiness is by way of an internal epiphany."

"Yes. I often wonder what sort of world it would be if more people felt as you and I."

"Perhaps there would never have been a war."

"And if no war, then perhaps no godless government in charge of Russia."

"I know only nightmares from the war. I saw a field of dead soldiers. I even witnessed the murder of a soldier."

"I was once in a village where there were hundreds of people—men, women, and children—all suffering from either typhus, typhoid, dysentery, or smallpox. I witnessed a dozen people dying each day."

I think to myself how much we have in common but how much of our lives have been filled with pain and suffering.

"Forgive me." She places a hand on my arm. "I think I must sound as though I am trying to one-up you as far as life experiences, but that is furthest from my mind." She sighs. "It is a funny thing."

"What is?"

"They are busy electing women to their parliament in England while here we're struggling to embrace the very concept of individual freedom."

While pondering her observation, I feel compelled to share with her my misgivings about Cassandra's involvement with revolutionaries and that she may be, at this very moment, aiding a movement to overthrow the government. She looks at the apartment door, and, rather than being displeased, she assures me there are certainly greater ongoing efforts in more clandestine venues than her tiny apartment. I hope, for her sake, that is truly the case.

❧

*October 1919*

Fall has a way of bringing on a sense of finitude, while winter, I imagine, will create some sort of a conclusion. There is an end approaching, but what it will be made up of, I cannot say. Each new day brings with it more bad news. Purging of political dissenters continues throughout the city long after the removal and execution of Tsar Nicholas II. What has changed? Nothing. Those now in power continue to exert their strength and authority by way of the same methods: cruelty and deprivation.

Cassandra's meetings in the shadows, to my mind, only serve to undermine Alexandra's efforts to locate my son. The three of us remain ensconced in the little apartment, but Cassandra's thoughts are distant, her despairing eyes filled with an obsession for something that can never be retrieved. I sense at times she has traveled back in time, back to when her life was filled with entitlement.

Alexandra suggests, for appearance's sake, we all attend the anniversary of the October Revolution. "The Square will be filled with supporters, the streets lined with throngs of obedient citizens cheering for the fledgling regime." She sounds less than sincere and appears even less so as she stares out the window and into the grayness of the overcast day. It looks as though it may snow.

I notice Cassandra's eyes fill with concern. "Is that such a good idea?" she asks, her tone snapping.

"Why not?" I look deeper into her eyes. "Isn't it best to appear above reproach?"

Cassandra looks to me and then to Alexandra. She feigns a smile. "I suppose you're right."

At times, my interceding between the two of them makes me feel like a river flowing between meandering banks, first in one direction and then in the other.

Alexandra steps out and engages a neighbor. I take the opportunity to ask Cassandra why she is acting so suspicious.

"I need to be able to trust you, Nora."

"Of course. But what is it?"

"There could be trouble at the celebration." Her voice is a murmur.

"What kind of trouble?"

"I shouldn't say. It may put your life in danger."

"How so?" She looks at me cautiously. "You must tell me, Cassandra."

"There could be violence."

"But why? How do you know this?" My mind begins to race. I instantly conclude the only way Cassandra could know of future events is because she is playing a part in them.

"I've said too much already. I shouldn't have told ... "

We're both startled as we hear Alexandra return. Cassandra looks at me, her face pleading for my discretion.

❧

The morning of the celebration finds Cassandra missing, without a word, from the apartment. I lie and tell Alexandra she is meeting friends.

"You know, Nora, I believe your friend to be an intellectual, but sometimes I wonder if she is capable of partaking in counter-revolutionary activities."

I say nothing. Of course, I know she has engaged in such activities both in the past and at present.

I feel an obligation to be at Alexandra's side as we trudge along on our way to Red Square. I know not what to expect but know that I could never forgive myself for allowing her to be placed in danger.

The people gathering around us along our walk appear to lack enthusiasm, considering the occasion. This is the second anniversary of the beginning of the "great experiment." The celebration, to my mind, is a mere pretense, as civil war rages on in other parts of the country in spite of the government's downplaying or outright censorship of the situation.

"Look." As we enter the square, Alexandra points in the direction of the Cathedral of Saint Basil to the east of the Kremlin citadel.

"Such beauty." The entire structure appears barbaric, yet majestic, like something out of the Abbasid era. Its domes stand tall like colorful onions against the gray sky and the Kremlin's tower spires.

The orderly crowd continues to grow both in size and din while a band plays one anthem after another. I search for Cassandra but realize it is futile.

Alexandra tugs at my wrist. "Let's get a closer look at this Lenin."

I allow her to pull me closer to the platform, weaving our way through the crowd. I can feel through her grasp that she is filled not with admiration but rather an aggressive strength. I wonder if she intends to use me as a club to beat Lenin. I want to resist but find myself equally interested in gaining access to the new leader. I have seen pictures of him and thought his face to be almost demonic in appearance, his mustache and goatee lacking only the accompaniment of a set of horns.

The crowd begins to compress, barring our advancement. The crowd around the front and sides of the stage is made up mostly of uniformed guards. We stand firm and listen. All around me, the faces are engaged by Lenin's rhetoric. He critiques the bourgeoisie, the exploiters, and the faux democrats, who continue to attempt to drive a wedge between the "haves" and the "have-nots." I am not in total disagreement but refrain from applause, as I know this is godlessness at the core.

The people appear entranced as Lenin's blustering billows through the atmosphere, yet I feel alone in an ocean of statues and begin to wonder what has become of Cassandra. I think back to our train ride so many years ago, when she described the means by which someone becomes an assassin. A welling of anxiety passes up through my lungs as I now allow the notion of Cassandra as assassin to slowly slip out of the back of my mind and rest in a whisper on the tip of my tongue. "Cass—"

At that moment, I hear a muffled crackling and then the sound of something like shattering glass. But there are no windows nearby. I look to the stage and see several men cautiously step nearer Lenin, wrapping around him and forming a safety shield. There is a burst of commotion to the right of the stage, where people are beginning to divide, while we at a distance strain to see what is going on. The interruption is instantly contained, and Lenin continues on as though nothing has occurred.

I stand dumbfounded, as does Alexandra. I listen with both awe and interest, realizing that such a little man can hold the attention of a multitude. A procession of dignitaries follows. The crowd roars "hurrah" while proudly waving. I now sense the overwhelming power of faith and trust so many have invested in one man. I am certain beyond belief that I do not belong here.

I sense Alexandra's nervousness as we walk back to the apartment. "What do you make of that?" I ask.

"I foresee more trouble." She begins to walk quickly as if she is attempting to create distance between us.

Later that evening, Cassandra shows herself. She appears both agitated and nervous. The three of us share a quiet yet uncomfortable evening.

❧

"I have bad news, ladies." Alexandra instantly piques our curiosity three days after the anniversary celebration.

After several months' worth of subtle inquiries, Alexandra informs me she has reached only dead ends with regard to the whereabouts of my son. She also informs us that, as commissary, she must return to Yasnaya Polyana by week's end.

I express my gratefulness while concealing my concern for this sudden decision.

I hear Cassandra sigh. "Yes. It is for the best that we move on."

Cassandra and I pack to make our way north to the Dukhobor settlement.

"I can give you some currency for the journey. It's not much, but the days of excess—for better or worse—are long gone for the House of Tolstoy."

I gladly take the money, as there is barely a ruble between Cassandra and myself. "It is a small fortune. Thank you." I am filled with guilt as I imagine I am leaving Alexandra at the mercy of Cassandra's conspirators and the secret police. "We will leave at first light for the station."

"The store shelves are usually empty, so you may find it hard to spend it. Good luck to you both."

# Blessed Are Those Who Are Persecuted

Blessed are those who are persecuted because of righteousness, for theirs is the kingdom of heaven.

Matthew 5:10

Cassandra and I trudge our way through Moscow, noting the pallor and chill of this once congenial city. During the tsar's reign, Saint Petersburg maintained a majestic air in light of squalor and oppression while Moscow was like a good-natured sister, filled with the promise of *Art Nouveau*, the Bolshoi Theatre, by example symbolic of the possibilities of progress. But then there is war, followed by a revolution, and now Moscow, and no doubt Saint Petersburg as well, are both shells of their greatness.

The faces we pass appear sallow and empty, taking on a sort of relaxed intimidation or resignation to fear, a stark difference from those I saw during the previous day's celebration. I am convinced we will blend in with the others as we pass through bureaucratic checkpoints.

With train tickets secured for Tomsk, we board, but I feel the heaviness of a set of eyes upon me. Alexandra's trials with the new government and Cassandra's subversive behavior both lend to my paranoia. I am in awe of this as I imagine how unlikely it would be for such a ubiquitous force as the government to ever consider helping me find my son but realize how involved it is in the lives of ordinary people for its own sake.

While the train rolls along, I think about one of many highbrow conversations I shared with Andre over the years. He had told me to look at the faces of the people you see, anywhere and anytime, and, generally, they are filled with muted indifference. He believed that most people were not interested in facing their greatest fear: death. As I sit here now and stare around the car, I think he was quite wrong. Yes. Muted indifference may be one interpretation, but I think, under the current climate, it is more of a combination of fear of the unknown and acceptance of what may come.

*November 1919*
Cassandra and I reach the settlement just as the weather changes from rain to sleet. We slip into camp quietly and announce ourselves to the first people we come across. We're greeted with caution. This is to be understood.

We're given fresh bread with potato soup. It is good to eat so heartily after so many days of traveling and scrounging for food in the woods.

The settlement is well maintained and, according to the leader, able to thrive in spite of the interference of the Cheka.

"It is most irregular for people to appear in the settlement out of nowhere." The spiritual head of the community does not provide reassurance. "This may become an issue when the Cheka arrive, as they maintain an iron clamp on the region. I don't need to tell you that the settlement, as well as others throughout the region, has lost favor since the overthrow of the government by the Bolsheviks."

"And when do you expect the Cheka?" I hear the exasperation in my voice. "Couldn't you hide us before they arrive?"

"They show up any time they like. Of course, we will attempt to hide you. But this is a task we will need to undertake until the spring, at which time, we should be able to find you safe passage into Scandinavia."

"We would be most grateful."

"Not at all. We owe a great debt to the late count for all that he did for those of our people who migrated to Canada twenty years ago. Is it truly your intent to flee to Scandinavia? I gather you have no desire to join the settlement."

"I would say I am more interested in locating my son; to this point, my efforts have been fruitless. Beyond that, my future remains uncertain."

"Well, you shall find both security and safety here for as long as is permitted."

I am already imagining how long and tedious another winter will be under the Bolsheviks.

The New Year is only two-weeks old when we learn Alexandra has been arrested by the Soviets and thrown in prison on the charge of plotting against the state. Thankfully, it is also noted that there are doubts of her being put to death because she is so well-known abroad.

I think to confront Cassandra, to admonish, but I find her continually deflating emotional state disarming. Most days, she bears with upright dignity the toiling labor we have signed on to, but I now see she is only a scant reflection of her old self. I remember how well she used to wear the garb of a true bohemian artist, like a beautiful peasant able to persuade others to manage the tasks of the day either by whimsy or cajoling. But here, no one is above the duties placed upon each individual and which are necessary to sustain the communal organism.

*April 1920*
Today, we find ourselves engaged in a laundry game. The spring thaw allows us the use of this little unnamed tributary to the River Tom to wash clothes and linens. We find the flow of water creates a sort of mechanized agitator as it weaves between the rocks along the shore. Cassandra drops a garment into the water upstream while I wait for it to worm its way down to where I am standing. Yakov, a new member to the settlement, stands, somewhat unsecure, on rocks a few paces from shore, holding a long pole. As the garment arrives downstream, Yakov allows me to drop the garment on the end while he hands it back to Cassandra to repeat the process.

I see Cassandra's smugness. It has been a long time since she has shown an interest in life. "Why should we overexert ourselves when the river can do its share?"

I can only smile as I suspect this little game only extends the time we will spend doing laundry, as some of the filthier linens will not be so easily cleaned by this new process. "If nothing else, it is interesting to see how and which way things will churn through this little nature-made labyrinth."

"I still prefer the old days when servants did these chores."

"Oh, come now. You know you would just be holed up in some stuffy parlor instead of outside enjoying the crisp air of this fine spring day."

"Ha! No doubt such was the case all your years at Yasnaya Polyana."

"Indeed."

"And the count scrubbing hard right beside you and Andre."

Yakov speaks softly. "Forgive me for prying. I remember this injured man whose name was Andre," he tells me with a face that is both thoughtful and at peace. "He told me he was from the estate of Tolstoy."

"Yes. He is my husband."

I am sorry to say that this man died back in July of last year."

I stand frozen. "How?" Yakov jabs the garment with the pole, pinning it against a rock before it escapes downstream. I reach down to retrieve the garment, unwilling to accept the news as fact. "Can you tell me what he looked like?"

Yakov describes Andre's brown eyes and his dark hair. He notes the birthmark on the back of his neck. "I only saw the birthmark after he removed his uniform shirt to reveal the large shrapnel wound on his back."

"You must tell me everything you know about him. I have not seen him for nearly six years." I place the garment on the end of the pole while staring out over the stream.

"It is a sad story."

"Please. I need to know for my own piece of mind." I see Yakov stumble on the rocks and look over at Cassandra, scolding, tugging at the pole. "It is okay, Cassandra. It is news I have been waiting for."

"But to learn under such circumstances. I should go away."

"As you wish."

Cassandra leaves Yakov and me alone by the stream, seated on rocks that have warmed under the noon sun. I brace myself and swallow hard while imagining the stream filled with my tears and, as such, convince myself I have no more to shed.

"Very well. I did not know him personally. He was in my unit from the beginning, but we were not familiar. If you'll permit me to say, I felt he was a very angry man, and I did not wish to associate with him on a personal basis. We became close when I helped to bring him back to the unit for medical attention, this after we had been ordered to take a small village that had been captured by the Germans. As our unit made its way across a level-plowed field during the summer night, I could feel the tension brewing as we neared the village. The night sky alternated between darkness and light as the clouds intermittently passed beneath the moon. Suddenly, I heard bullets flying by, over and over. Everyone fell to the ground and began to fire toward the village.

"We were able to out-flank the Germans but at the cost of many lives. And by morning, we were able to take the village after many German soldiers surrendered. It is at this time that I came across Andre wandering around. He asked me to wrap his wound. That is when he removed his bloody shirt, and I saw that his wound was too large for me to wrap. As he and I made our way back to the unit, we came across trenches filled with dead German soldiers. I heard the cries of one soldier from the trench begging for help. I went to help but saw that he had a leg wound that was more than I could deal with. He begged my help in German, but I expressed my regret by placing my hand on my chest and shaking my head with sadness. I gave him a drink of water from my flask.

"Andre and I continued walking down the road. He was very thirsty, and his steps were labored. As he drank from my flask, I offered my shoulder for him to lean against. Just as he was about to take my shoulder, he collapsed to the ground. I knelt down before him and told him it was not much farther. But he was fading away before my eyes. He said, 'the master was right.' He said this several times. Then he told me, 'I have made a grave mistake, comrade.' I tried to jest with him, tried to lift his spirits and tell him how we're at war and being led by officers and, as such, we soldiers, one and all, have made a mistake. 'No,' he tells me. 'My mistake is that I have left a good woman and my son all alone to fight and die for no good reason.' I tell him how we're fighting for the Fatherland, but this does nothing to lift his spirits.

"I begged him to hold on as he lay on his back, prone like a man readying himself for the end. His breathing became labored. He knew he was finished and asked me one favor. 'Please send word to Nora Nelsonova at Yasnaya Polyana and tell her of my love for her and my son, Teodor, and my shame for having left them behind.' Then he said no more.

"I did send word after the war but received no reply. Obviously, you did not get my letter."

"I'm afraid not, Yakov. There has been much chaos since. But I thank you for your efforts and for telling me of Andre's last moments."

I am bereft but do not want to make Yakov feel uncomfortable. I ask him to tell me his own story. He is more than willing to share it with me, for which I am grateful, as he has become my last link to Andre. He is thirty-five years old, five years younger than me, but he sounds like someone who has lived twice that length.

"I was like a dumb animal, a sheep," he says, telling about his life of debauchery and of his excessive drinking. "I could not find my way in life. I was a constant disappointment to my parents. I had two brothers who made good in life. One brother went to university and became a successful businessman in Petrograd, while the other advanced up the ranks in the military. But I could not find my way."

I could see he was wearing the remnants of a military uniform. "Did you not advance in the military, Yakov?"

"No. I was too undisciplined. I was actually conscripted and had no interest in being in the military. I spent much of the time in the guardhouse, usually because of drunkenness."

"Why so much drink?"

"Looking back, I'm not sure, but I remember being taught to fight and to be ready to kill all enemies foreign and domestic in the name of the tsar, the fatherland, and the faith. This frightened me, but the idea of being taught to kill was not as overwhelming as the actual killing that was to come when Russia and Germany were at war. I can tell you, Nora, I was very afraid of being killed but also of killing someone. I guess I found much solace in drinking."

"So how did you finally find your way here?"

"It was after the war that I began to read the writings of Tolstoy. I was moved by his beliefs in non-violence and how he attributed them to Christ's Sermon on the Mount."

⁂

*November 1920*

It appears Cassandra and I may never leave Russia. It is a year since our arrival, and our escape has been postponed on several occasions due to one obstruction or another. Each time I have agreed with the spiritual leader that it is best to err on the side of caution. There is no telling how far we might have gone with increasingly vigilant checkpoints and patrols. This makes sense any other day except for today.

The Cheka arrives today, enveloping the community in a blanket of fear. While we're rounded up for interrogation, I spot a face among the soldiers that possesses the features of my Teodor. I am apt to shout out but think twice about doing so for fear of placing both he and Cassandra in danger. Now I must find a way to avoid drawing attention to myself while making eye contact with my son.

The interrogating has gone on all day, and it is late in the afternoon when there is a commotion in the square. The soldiers are gathering all the men from the settlement together.

"It looks like the cat and mouse game has concluded," says Cassandra. "Now I fear the worst is about to happen."

The head Cheka officer demands everyone's attention. "If you will not swear allegiance to the state and join the rest of your comrades in serving the collective, then we will use other methods of persuasion."

Every tenth man is singled out and ordered to kneel in the center of the square, and all the women are forced to watch as scalding water is poured down each man's throat. There is both fear and trembling in the air, but it is overshadowed by faith in God's will.

Now the women are gathered, and proof of identification is demanded of all. My son stands near me during this process. There is an air of uncertainty as each woman presents her papers. As I hand my documents to the headman, I look at my son, who will only show me an occasional glance out of the corner of his eye. I want to run to him and embrace him tightly, but instead, I only feel a need to conceal my emotions so as not to put either of our lives in danger. The headman hands my papers back to me. Cassandra steps into my place and hands her documents forward. As I begin to walk away, I hear him say, "Ah, yes. We've been looking high and low for you, Cassandra Grigoravich." I stop dead in my tracks and think twice about spinning around to defend my friend or taking her by the arm and making a dash for the forest. Then I think how we might be shot down like dogs, and I wonder if my Teodor would be compelled out of duty to fire on us as well. "And this is your travel companion?" he now asks. I know he is referring to me, as I stand firm, the stiffness of my back betraying me.

"That is not my last name," Cassandra responds. "And I have traveled alone. I arrived here alone."

"Is that your story, Cassandra Grigoravich?"

"It is the truth."

Then I hear a slap and quickly turn around. I can see the headman is about to strike Cassandra again. "I am with her. She is my friend."

The headman looks at us and waves to the two attending soldiers. "Arrest these two."

My son rushes over to me, not to embrace me, but rather to bind my hands while the other soldier does the same to Cassandra.

We're thrown in the back of a wagon. I gather Cassandra to me and console her. It is cold and damp, and light breaks through the roof, but only when we pass through open spaces along the road. Otherwise, the trees lay heavy upon us like a boot belonging to the Soviet government. My only source of comfort is the knowledge that my Teodor accompanies us on our journey to God knows where.

During two brief stops, I can see someone peering in through the cracks in the side boards of the wagon. I am certain it is my son. I wish to call out to him but think it best not to, for his sake.

⚜

We're taken to the nearest village, Yurga, and thrown in a cell where four other women are being held. Cassandra and I sit in a corner farthest from the door. I think back to when she and I first met and how strong in spirit she was then. Now, she seems to be lost to all things worldly. A terrible idea begins to rise in my thoughts. Would I lose yet another friend to despair?

We're greeted with both apprehension and interest by the other women. One of them approaches us, introducing herself as a civil servant from Petrograd who has been betrayed by a fellow worker. She explains how, one day while she was working, secret documents were placed in her possession. She is accused of spying for the Whites.

"Why are you here?" the woman asks.

"Say nothing," says Cassandra. "She may still be a spy."

"Oh, you mean like her?" The woman points to another woman who is curled up in the corner nearest the door. Her hair is scraggy and her gray clothes weathered. "The rest of us taught her a lesson. Three days ago, we caught her fraternizing with one of the guards. She won't be crossing us again."

"Is it true?" I ask the others.

A woman whose face has been in a constant state of sadness since our arrival says, "I heard her speaking to the guard, telling him about our conversations."

A third woman nods.

"So you see," says the civil servant, kneeling down before us, "we do not have a problem with spies in our cell." Then she looks directly at Cassandra, who still bows her head. "Your friend should look to us for help. We are all here together, so we should make the best of things."

Without looking up, Cassandra says, "Trust no one, Nora."

❧

The interrogator asks me, "Are you familiar with the name Alexandra Tolstoy?"

"Of course I have heard of that name. She is the daughter of the famous writer, Leo Tolstoy."

"And when did you last speak with her?"

I sit there, considering how best to respond.

"It's a simple question, Ms. Thorsen. Perhaps the month and year?"

"Late November or early December of this past year."

"And what was the nature of your conversation?"

"Nothing that would concern you or the government."

"Let me correct you. Your activities are of great interest to the Soviets, as there is an abundance of evidence indicating that you have conspired with at least one known enemy of the state and at least one suspected enemy of the state."

"I'm sure there are many Russian citizens who associate with people on a daily basis that may have ties to revolutionaries, but that does not mean they are revolutionaries themselves."

"That may be true, but surely you can appreciate the need for the police to take as much time as needed and to take all precautions necessary to ensure that all such people are either found guilty by association or innocent by extenuating circumstances."

"Sir, I am not a revolutionary."

"Then what is your business so far from Tula?"

"I am in search of my son."

"Ah, yes. It says here that you have an eighteen-year old son named Teodor Thorsen. He does not go by his father's name?"

I had insisted on Teodor taking my last name when we filed for documentation to leave the country before the war. "His father was lost to us many years ago."

"I see. Perhaps if you answer my questions, I can help you find your son?"

The interrogator's suggestion takes me by surprise, and I am not sure how I should respond. I ask questions I think might allow me time to consider things. "Exactly what information are you looking for?"

"As I say, we know you are very much linked to Miss Cassandra Grigoravich. What I need to know is what knowledge you have about her revolutionary activities?"

I stare just above the man's head. I think less about what I know, which is virtually nothing, as I had insisted Cassandra not tell me of such things, but more so how I would have answered had I actually had knowledge of her activities. Would I have felt compelled to answer for the sake of being with my son once again? Deciding that it is a moot point, I answer his question directly. "Would you believe me if I told you I have nothing incriminating to say about Miss Grigoravich?"

"No, I would not. And furthermore, I think you are making an unwise decision. Miss Grigoravich's fate has already been decided, but yours could be less drastic with your cooperation."

"I'm sure you'll understand, sir, how it would be beneath me to create a fiction for the sole purpose of saving myself from a fate you are suggesting."

After several hours of interrogation, I am allowed to return to the cell. There I find Cassandra still curled in the corner, but this time, she appears even smaller than before. I kneel before her, and she looks at me and whispers, "I am a dead woman."

"So am I," I whisper as well, holding her close.

Again, I think of how broken Cassandra appears when compared to our liveliness so many years ago. And even in our hour of desperation, I feel content and without regret, but I realize Cassandra could not find any solace in anything I say. I remind her of her family and her promising career as a woman artiste.

"No, Nora. I have wasted my life. I was an unruly child and an undisciplined painter. But worse than anything, I am a malcontented revolutionary, and now I am to die for reasons I cannot understand."

"Don't give up hope, my dear. This cannot be an entirely unlawful land. There must be recourse somehow and somewhere in Russia."

"I envy your outlook. If only I had the faith of Nora." That she speaks not to me but to someone invisible gives me hope that Cassandra's heart and soul are ready for the final journey.

We have been locked away for several weeks. We have no idea when we will be leaving for someplace more obscure and distant. Our cellmate, the civil servant, describes the typical slow death of a political prisoner involving years of hard labor far away at some outpost in a Siberian gulag. "Death will come when death has decided. I know. I maintained the paperwork for several cases."

I consider myself a person quite patient with most people, but to be confined to a cell with five women grows tedious. I have learned all I wish to know about everyone and now would prefer to remain isolated. Even Cassandra's dispiritedness leaves me feeling somewhat contemptuous. I search for hope and meaning, but these luxuries seem to be reserved for those who are carefree.

I have restrained myself from incriminating my son in my plight, as I feel it makes no sense to put his life in danger for the sake of a mother's yearning to speak and hold her son. But how I wish I could get word to him through the guards. He knows I am here; if he could only find a way to see me. I think how controlling the new government is and conclude that perhaps my own son is more an instrument of the system and less a son. The maxim that a brother is duty-bound to betray a brother for the sake of the collective does little to lift my hopes that my son is still my son.

⚜

It is morning, and the barred, translucent window that sits high near the ceiling barely allows the entry of the light from what must be a brilliant sunrise. There is the usual anticipation of being served breakfast. It is an empty joy that serves mostly to break up the monotony of the day while providing a sense of time.

As the cell door opens, the guard walks in with his head bowed. We have had several guards at different times, but this appears to be a new guard. Something inside me tells me to look at this man's face. As is usual, the guard sets our pot of gruel and bowls in the middle of the room. Cassandra and I both begin to move toward the pot. The guard steps past Cassandra and walks to the window. He briefly looks up at it and then turns with his back toward me. I now realize it is Teodor, even as he begins to stand with his back between the cell door and me, as I remain seated on the floor in the corner. He quickly tosses to me a rolled-up piece of paper. I catch it and quickly conceal it in my blouse. He leaves as quickly as he came.

I scurry up to the pot of gruel so as not to draw attention to what has occurred. All are hungry and begin to eat with purpose. I quickly join in, hoping my eyes do not betray me.

"What was the guard doing at the window?" The civil servant creates a curiosity among my cellmates.

"I don't know. But he was blocking my way."

The sad-looking woman says a sad thing. "I wonder if he found the window allowing too much light in and will now report it to his superior."

"Undoubtedly," I agree, hoping to put an end to the subject, but the civil servant continues to search my face. Now the joy I have is replaced with fear.

It is several hours before I dare read the note. As I quietly unroll it, I make sure the others, even Cassandra, are napping. I need to read it quickly, for I know there could come a time when a knock on the door would rouse everyone. Interrogations are ongoing, even for the condemned.

I cradle the note in my hand and read the few lines scribbled on it.

*I COME FOR YOU THIS NITE*

*STAY CLOSE TO THE DOOR*

A small cell with so many people is not an easy place to hide secrets. It is difficult to tell Cassandra Teodor's instructions.

"But what if he intends to help only you?"

"Nonsense. I will let him know you are coming as well."

"But where would we go?"

"I've no idea where. But would not any place be more preferable to here?"

"I'm not so sure."

"Don't be silly. You'll come with me to America."

"I know that was your intention when we first came north, but I am not so certain that I can have a new life in such a far-off land."

"What are you saying?" asks the sad-faced woman. "Do you have news from the outside? You must share it."

"We're only reminiscing," I say, raising my voice. "Can't two people reminisce without an inquisition?" The sad-faced woman looks away, but the civil servant looks to us out of the corner of her eye.

"I think it will be hard for me to leave Russia."

"But why?"

"This is my homeland. I think there is much to fight for here. It would feel as though I were running away just when I am needed most to help defend the people's liberties."

"How can you do that in a labor camp?"

"You're right, Nora. I think I am only fooling myself. I have squandered my life in luxury and privilege while you have made something of yours."

"And I intend to make even more of it, for the sake of God. I wish to return home with my son and to watch him live a good life, to marry, to give me grandchildren."

"Listen to the dreamers," says the civil servant.

"Don't you have dreams?" I ask.

"My dreams are the property of the Soviets. And so are yours."

"You are a contemptible, woman." Cassandra almost spits out the words. "I think you accept your fate either because you are guilty or because you are a spy."

"This spy nonsense again? I thought we cleared that matter up weeks ago."

"These days, you can never be a hundred percent sure of anyone's innocence."

Just then, we hear a scurrying noise near the corner of the ceiling.

"What is that?" asks the civil servant.

"Just more rats," answers the sad-faced woman.

"I don't think so." The civil servant now stands.

"I will look," I say, hoping to put an end to it. I step up on the edge of one of the pallets. I can reach my fist through a hole in the corner of the ceiling. "Lend me your hairbrush," I tell the civil servant, "so I can reach farther into the hole with the handle. Maybe I can make it go away."

I reach through the hole with the handle. Just then something takes hold of it. I dare not let loose of the brush and grip it tightly. Now it feels like the grip of someone's hand.

"Who are you?" I now hear a voice whispering.

"Who are you?" I whisper in return.

Then I lose hold of the hairbrush.

"What are they saying?" asks the civil servant.

"Nothing. But they've taken the hairbrush."

A moment or two later, I hear someone whisper, "Here."

I reach into the hole and grab the hairbrush. When I pull it back through, it has a piece of paper attached to it. I jump down from the pallet and begin unfolding it while looking in the direction of the cell door.

"What does it say?" asks Cassandra.

"It is a list of five names. It must be the names of those in the cell next door."

"That's strange," ponders Cassandra. "We have heard nothing from either side of the walls since we arrived."

"Maybe they were jailed recently."

"We should give them our names in return," says the civil servant, "as a sign of trust."

Cassandra is now animated as she stands directly in front of the civil servant. "Are you stupid or a spy? Why do you consider trust so easy to come by under these circumstances?"

"All I am saying is that we are all prisoners and can help each other."

"Yes. Help each other get into more trouble or to increase the amount of distrust that already exists."

"Cassandra," I begin, "there is no harm in exchanging names with our neighbors. If nothing else, it is polite." She then walks back and sits in the corner of the cell. For this, I am glad, as I wish not to draw the guard's attention. "I will write down all of our names and pass it over."

The civil servant continues to pace back and forth across the cell, insistent that something should occur.

"What can we tell them?" she asks.

"I don't know. You know as much as I." I begin to jest. "Perhaps we could form an alliance with them and attempt to create an elaborate plot to escape."

"Is it possible?"

I feel uneasy and quickly say, "No, of course not."

"I know you," Cassandra interrupts.

"What?" The civil servant asks.

"I know you," she repeats.

I retreat to the corner where it feels comfortable and safe. There has been too much activity, and I am anxious for nightfall. Cassandra sits in front of me, just to my right. It is as though she is positioning herself between the civil servant and me.

The light has been out for what must be several hours. Cassandra and I are seated on the floor next to the door when we here cautious footsteps. I think how it must be Teodor. I rouse Cassandra, whose head rests on my lap.

"I am awake," she says.

"What is it?" asks the civil servant.

"What is what?" I whisper. She is still awake. I now realize she suspects something is afoot.

"Why are you by the door? Are you leaving?"

"You shut up," says Cassandra in a snapping whisper.

"I am ill," says the civil servant. "I need to see the guard."

"Rubbish!" Cassandra lurches forward.

"Guard!"

"Shut up, you!"

"Stop it. Both of you." I am becoming unnerved. The others begin to stir. I now hear footsteps approaching the cell door.

"Guard!" The civil servant's voice increases in volume, but just then, Cassandra leaps up. I hear shuffling of hands and feet and then the murmuring of someone followed by gagging. A key penetrates the cell door lock. I begin to panic, believing the escape plan has been detected and foiled. Light from the hallway breaks into the cell. A dark silhouette stands just outside the doorway. I look over my shoulder to see Cassandra wrestling the civil servant to the floor.

"Mother!" I instantly recognize the voice in the doorway as Teodor's. "Come away."

"I will hold this one down if it takes me all night." I can make out in the darkness Cassandra's arms and legs wrapped around the civil servant's lower body as they lay on the floor.

"We must go, Cassandra!"

"We must go, Mother!"

"My friend must come with us, Teodor."

"Which one?"

"No, Nora. You must leave now with your son. I cannot let this spy go free until you are far away."

"You are choking her to death."

"That is her choice. As long as she keeps her mouth shut, I will let her breathe."

"Mother, we must hurry!"

"Cassandra! Come with us. You can be free."

"No, Nora. I have never been free, even when I was not in jail. I did not know how to live free. You are much better at it than I. Now go."

Teodor pulls me through the door, his strength much greater than when we last touched. I am unable to look back at my lost friend and, instead, am whisked down the hallway.

I see a guard slumped over the desk as we pass by. We make our way outside into the darkness. There are two horses waiting for us. Teodor helps me mount, and we quietly and slowly make our way through the village, heading in the direction of the mountain range.

There is a checkpoint at the end of the village. Teodor tells me, "You must act like my mother."

"But I am your mother."

"Is that you, Andreovich?" asks the sentry.

"It is I, Pavel, but who else?"

"You are off duty so early. And who is that with you?"

"My mother. She is up from the Caucauses visiting relatives in the village. I am escorting her to her sister's farm just down the road. I will return."

"It is very late, madam."

"Good evening, officer."

"Ha! Your mother knows little about the military. I am not an officer, madam. They are a clever bunch who would never find themselves standing outside in the dark guarding against fox and rabbit."

There is a momentary pause as the sentry shifts from one foot to the other. "I will say good night to you, madam."

We continue on our way. It just now dawns on me that Teodor has taken back his father's name after returning to Russia. And I have lost another dear, old friend.

# The Lord Will Keep You from All Harm

The LORD will keep you from all harm—
he will watch over your life; the LORD will
watch over your coming and going both now
and forevermore.

Psalm 121:7–8

*February 1921*

"How do we know you can be trusted? Already you have placed the entire settlement in jeopardy." The spiritual leader is beside himself with anger.

Teodor is equally vehement in his response. "You people speak of the collective. Are we not part of the collective?"

"How can *you* speak of such things? You were here, only weeks ago, with the Cheka to both persecute and purge. There is a chasm between our community and the *collective* you are a part of."

"It is my mother I live for now. Before I found my mother, I was merely a tool for the Bolsheviks because I had no other meaning for living."

"But now you come here, and you will most certainly be followed."

"What other choice did we have? I know only you people, who are of the same mind as my mother."

"But how can we keep you or help you to get away?"

"Couldn't you smuggle us in with others immigrating to Canada?"

"Do you really think that would be fair to them? It is from state-sponsored persecution they wish to legally flee from, and here you are, suggesting they risk freedom by aiding and abetting fugitives?"

"Forgive me, sir. But as you so succinctly point out, I have just deserted from the army and am no doubt wanted for the unlawful release of a prisoner. Surely you can afford me a bit of reckless thinking."

The leader nods at Teodor while contemplating our circumstances. "Your best chance is to make your way to Finland through the Ural Mountains. That is over one-thousand miles. But even then, you will encounter many checkpoints. It is a struggle enough for a young man, but your mother may not endure."

"I will do whatever it takes to get out of Russia with my son."

"Very well. I will make arrangements for a sledge and provisions so that you may leave immediately. But please keep in mind that I will speak freely to the authorities once they arrive."

"What do you mean?"

"I will tell them you were here and where you are going."

I can see the anger in Teodor's eyes as he looks at the leader. "That is best," I begin explaining to him. "We have jeopardized this community enough by our presence."

Teodor is anxious as he harnesses the two stolen military steeds to the sledge. It is very early in the morning, and the sun is beginning to rise. The chill in the air is tantamount to a bucket of icy water thrown in the face. With so many miles to travel, I am weary of what awaits us in the wilderness as well as the brutality of the Soviet government should we be captured.

Teodor explains how the sledge will move roughly but quickly over much of the terrain between the settlement and the Urals. Even so, we will be out in the open and in view of search parties.

We spend the first day making great progress. We have been provided with a good map. Teodor estimates we have already covered fifty miles, a daily average, I surmise, which would mean we should see the border of Finland in less than a month. But now he reminds me how our pace over the Urals will be much slower and how we will need to secure provisions along the way, as we're only carrying a week's worth.

"This will not be easy, Mama. I hope you understand what is at stake." His voice is stern, almost accusatory.

"Of course."

"Our lives."

"I know this." I meet his tone with equal sternness. "I have put my life at risk these past many months for the sake of finding you. Do you honestly believe that I do not understand the danger we find ourselves in?"

Teodor's voice, now tempered, begins to speak of the past. He apologizes for running away from me and explains how it was necessary for him to return to his homeland and to fight alongside his Russian brothers. He tells me of his service time spent on the frontline witnessing the cruelty of both the Germans and the

Russians. I am shocked when he denounces the existence of a god.

I tell him, dispassionately, how difficult the past years were without knowledge of his whereabouts and whether or not he was still alive. I'm sure he hears above the subtle scolding my joy in our reuniting under the most incredible circumstances. I tell him how my trust in God sustained me. There is only the future, and I have found my son. I consider telling him of the fate of his father.

The cold air is in some strange way comforting. Of course, the warm coats and blankets my son and I share are equally comforting, but I imagine how our pursuers must be experiencing greater comfort, as there is no risk in their creating a fire to secure warmth. This will, undoubtedly, work to their advantage, making our capture much easier.

Teodor tells me what will happen should we be captured. He tells of prison camps made especially for criminals and political prisoners alike. The work is unbearable, as men spend, in some cases, up to sixteen hours a day hauling and stacking logs on to barges or filling, by hand, train cars with chunks of coal. This is based on stories he has heard from his connections to the Cheka. He cannot speak for the women under similar circumstances but assures me it is no more pleasant an existence than that of the men.

I ponder the wisdom of man, as I have so often. How does evil maintain its grip on the world in light of such great teachers as Christ and the master?

It becomes necessary for Teodor to break ice on the nearby river so that the horses can drink. It is a laborious task and slows our travel. The horses are able to forage in the lowlands, but we both worry about how well they will survive as we ascend through the Urals. Our lives depend on the lives of our horses.

On our third day, a Siberian tiger begins to parallel our trail. It is the first sign of life we have seen thus far. It is a marvelous-looking beast that bounces through the snow with what appears to be curiosity and playfulness. Teodor moves the horses along, trying to maintain a steady clip while avoiding a sudden change in movement. After a short time, we notice the gap is growing smaller between the tiger and the sledge. I can now clearly see its marbled eyes, filled with determination, while its jaw hangs with a look of ravenousness. Teodor decides we must risk detection by firing rifle shots at the tiger before it becomes brazen enough to attack the horses. I now hold the reins while Teodor readies his rifle. Just then a pack of wolves—perhaps seven or eight in all—rush down from out of the forest, descending upon the tiger. It stops to stand its ground. Teodor takes the reins back from me and hurries the horses. Like him, I too sense the opportunity to get away, far from the tiger, while avoiding the wolves' attention.

As I look back, I can see the tiger swatting with heavy paws at the wolves as they surround him. Our distance increases more as the tiger runs in the opposite direction from us, taking with him the pack of wolves.

---

It is late in the day as the sun, still high, starts to set. It has been hours since our encounter with the tiger and the wolves.

I begin to tell Teodor of my experience with the unruly black bear from when I was a young girl.

"Mama, I have heard this story a thousand times."

"Does it bore you?"

"Yes, it is a very old, boring tale. Even though you add new pieces to it—I suspect you are trying to spice it up from the previous telling—it is still a very worn-out story."

"But a bear that is crazy. Do you know of another bear that is crazy enough to climb onto the roof of a house and try to climb down the chimney?"

Teodor sighs. "No, Mama. That is a crazy bear, indeed."

"Why not break in the front door?" I raise my arms in bewilderment.

"Why not blow the house down, crazy bear?" a grouchy Teodor asks.

"That is the big bad wolf you are thinking of."

"Oh, yes. I knew there was a tale of another crazy animal."

---

It has been a week without a sign of soldiers or Cheka agents. We reward our week-long efforts with a blazing fire, as the night air is bitterly cold. It will be nice to spend one night stretched out on the ground rather than cramped in the tiny compartment of the sledge.

I believe Teodor has become cavalier regarding our circumstances. "Are we so skilled in outmaneuvering our pursuers? Or have we been blessed with good luck?"

"It is the hand of God, my son. Without it, we would surely be lost in the vastness of this great land."

He looks at me as though I have sprouted the wings of an angel. I know he thinks me naïve and superstitious, but now that we're together again, I shall do whatever I can to help him to rekindle his faith.

We have been provided excellent directions and have located a trail through the Middle Urals that will provide expediency but risk of capture should we cross paths with anyone.

The journey is peaceful. The forest is calm.

We happen upon the village of Pokcha. A man named Haeivsky, acting as the town administrator, begs us to spend time in the village and to rest from our journey. This man is overweight and overbearing. Teodor shares my concerns regarding our host's insistence, but we're both too tired and weary. We're aware of the distrust that pervades the entire country, as citizens are duty bound to report suspicious travelers and activities, but we believe the horses need the rest, as there are still a full five hundred miles between the village and the Finnish border.

Haievsky suggests we lodge at a local tavern and inn where the accommodations are modest but comfortable and inexpensive. Along with a number of local denizens, there is a fellow traveler, a magician. His name is Brumel, but he insists everyone call him by his given name, Valery. He is of husky build with dark and curly hair, beard, and moustache. He performs tricks and tells the fortunes of the women. They pay him with food, fish, or milk.

"Might I tell you your fortune, young lady?"

"I'm sorry, but I have no means of payment."

"I will do it for free, if that is all right."

He takes my hand and reads the lines. "Ah, I see you and your son travel a far distance."

I look at Teodor, who sits nearby drinking a cup of local port. I frown at him. With a slight motion, he lurches forward. "Nephew."

Both the magician and I look quizzically at Teodor.

"This is my aunt," he explains. "And we do not travel so far. From Perm to Berezniki. It is not so far."

"Yes," I continue to explain, taking note of the pretense. "It is true. A very short journey." I pull my hand away. "Perhaps it is a confusing-looking palm?"

"Your people are from Perm?"

Teodor slouches matter-of-factly. "Everyone's people are from Perm."

"Of course." The magician smiles with agreement. "I have been to Berezniki. Perhaps I know the people you are visiting?"

"We know no one in Berezniki."

"Then why do you say you are traveling there?"

"We are meeting people." Teodor stretches his arms while arching his back. As he reaches for his cup, he says, "Perm people."

The magician begins to laugh while fluttering his fingers through his beard.

I smile but am certain I am betraying my anxiety and guilt. "I am tired, Nephew. I think I shall retire for the evening."

"Good night, Auntie." Teodor lifts his cup to me.

❧

I awake to the sound of muffled voices and shuffling footsteps outside the window of my little room. I rise, wrap a shawl around my shoulders, and step outside only to find two men entangled, aggressively pushing each other about while heavy snowflakes fall around them.

"Teodor!" The darkness forbids me from seeing the faces of the two figures struggling as if engaged in a silent dance. The silhouette now is that of one man standing behind the other and choking him. I hear gasping of the one above the angry grunting of the other. I am fearful for the man gasping. "Teodor!"

"Shut up!" Just as I am ready to intervene, the aggressor smashes the man's head into a wooden pole. I stand frozen in my steps, frightened by my inability to call out, and then he smashes the man's head again into the wooden pole, and his body goes limp. The assailant drops to the ground along with the man and continues to strangle him. Even so, the man has gone limp in his grasp.

Moments later, he lets go of his victim, who lies there motionless. The murderer stands for a moment while breathing hard and then begins to approach me. I try to look into his eyes, but it is too dark. He takes me by the wrist, pulling me away from the crime he has committed. "We must leave now." I can still feel the rage surging through his entire body. I try to break from his grip. I want to help the man lying on the ground.

"Who are you?" I tremble in both speech and body.

"Who am I?" The man pulls me closer to his face. I now see that it is Teodor, but he's not the son I remember. "You should be asking me who he was."

"Very well." I am able to relax to a degree. "Who was the man you just murdered?"

"He is a Bolshevik agent. He was about to arrest us while we slept."

"How do you know this?" I am filled with both fear and anger. I cannot bear to look at my son, the murderer. I have witnessed men dying in hospital from battle or from the result of disease. I think back to the German soldier's murder of the wounded French soldier. As cold blooded as that murder was, it has been easier for me to forget than will be this act by my own son.

"Late last night, after you had gone to bed, I followed this so-called magician and overheard both he and the administrator conspiring to arrest us. In fact, he is a prison camp administrator who is transporting two political prisoners to Edzhyt Kyrta, *White Mountain*."

"But to murder a man for this reason?"

"Mama, you need to set aside your high principles if we are to escape from Russia."

"I don't wish to murder our way out of here."

Now Teodor takes my hand in both of his, squeezing gently. I begin to grow submissive and allow him to lead the way.

We slip out of the village quietly and speak not another word as we make our way down the road, until it dawns on me to ask about the political prisoners. "What will become of them now that their escort is no longer alive?"

"I'm sure the town administrator will deal with them once he learns what has happened."

"But shouldn't we go back and set them free?"

"Mama. That would be very dangerous and foolish."

"But if we leave them to their fate, are we not equally guilty?"

"Do you mean in the eyes of God?"

"Of course."

"How can we help when we are fugitives ourselves? The whole country is filled with fugitives. We cannot help them all, Mama. Trust me. I have found myself in similar situations where I could not help my comrades."

I look at him quizzically.

He hesitates but then begins to explain. "The war found me fighting so many different enemies. At one point, I felt everyone was the enemy. Not to mention the barbarism I experienced."

"We should find the good in people, like Jesus did, no matter the circumstances."

"Easy to say but harder to do when you see your comrades buried upside down, up to their kneecaps, while their captors look on, sportingly, waiting to see who will be the last one kicking for his last breath." He appears reflective. "You may be right, but I think it is the event I must learn to despise rather than the people involved."

I begin to realize how wise my son has become over the years and how gray my own beliefs. He has the cunning sense of his father but, hopefully, also a little bit of the quiet compassion of his Norwegian mother.

We have avoided capture. We are home free. A fortnight goes by without incident. We have zigzagged our way through the Arkhangelsk region and the Republic of Karelia, bypassing Saint Petersburg by way of the northern route around Ladoga Lake. At last, we are in Finland.

We rest in a small camp whose members are made up of both Finnish and Russian sympathizers of the Whites. We are to be transported to the American consulate in Helsinki in the morning. It will be nice to be ensconced in the comfort of a city. I am tired of the wilderness, tired of the survivalist mentality it engenders, and tired of living as both predator and prey in a land besieged by constant conflict.

# The Kingdom of God Is Within You

Nor will people say, "Here it is," or "There it is," because the kingdom of God is within you.

Luke 17:21

*Summer 1921*

The softness of my old bed and the sound of springs give way to the weight of my still-slender figure. I think about the last time I was here in my old bedroom, over twenty years ago. All my brothers and sisters have long since moved on, leaving the upstairs of the old family farmhouse nothing more than a hulk of the past. Strips of wallpaper peel away from the ceiling corners like the years from my youth. I feel older and wiser, and the dreams of my youth are replaced by the experiences of a life lived and molded by the will of God.

I look up at the portrait, the painting, longing for the past while appreciating the present. There is guilt, but it has finally been overshadowed by repentance, by what I believe to be an amended life.

The feelings the painting brings me are different now compared to when I first set eyes on it so many years ago. I remember how Ella and I posed, how we had made allowances of modest impropriety for the artist, all for the prideful sake of immortality.

"I believe I have served your memory well," I conclude, staring up at the portrait. "And I will continue to do so for as long as I live." But just as I say the words, I feel a rush of doubt. I now find myself wondering if I have known what the meaning of it all really is.

*I am forty.* I realize my fortieth birthday is six months past just as my mother walks into the room, the old floor creaking under each step. All at once, I feel pity for my mother. "I've been gone so long, Mama. I can't believe how old I've let you become."

"I still feel the same as the day you left. Maybe even younger, now that you've returned."

"You never said in any of your letters, but how cruel you must have felt me to be when I chose to be away for so long."

"A mother never begrudges her child from living her own life."

I reach for my mother's hand. It feels cold and frail. My purity of sight fades, now clouded with doubt, as I kiss her hand. "Forgive me," I whisper.

I hear the slamming of the screen door downstairs. "Nora!" My father calls me from downstairs. "You have a visitor."

"I forgot to tell you." My mother places her hands to her face in shock. "We were so excited to see you when you arrived late last night that I forgot to tell you."

"Tell me what?"

"I'm not sure how to tell you this, dear daughter, but..."

"Nora?"

I see an apparition in the bedroom doorway. Time seems to stand still as I stare, transfixed by what is before my eyes. My breathing quickens, and I slide from the bed, falling to my knees, weeping with both joy and sadness. I sense my eyes are deceiving me. My mother is quickly by my side, lifting me to my feet and holding me up.

"Is it really you, Ella?" I ask.

"I am Nora," she answers.

"How?" I feel faint.

"I have a story to tell you and so many questions to ask you, but maybe not now. You do not look well."

I stand on my own and walk past the vision before me, my eyes measuring while my hand reaches to touch her cheek with suspicion. "I am all right, only very surprised by how much you look like my long departed friend."

"And it is amazing for me to finally meet the person who my name derives from."

"Who are you?" I step into the doorway, blocking the exit should this spirit decide to bolt.

"Hasn't anyone told you yet?" She looks at my mother. "I'm the daughter of Ella Pederson."

"How?" I reflect on how this can, and if true, why Ella would name her daughter after me, considering how I had treated her all those years ago. "But where do you come from?" I try not to sound impolite.

"I am from the Dukhobor settlement in British Columbia. I have lived there for the past twenty years."

I think about the time that has passed and how long I have been out of touch with my home. My mind is flooded with questions. "But how did you know where to find where your mother was from?"

"It wasn't easy, but I was able to trace your name— my name—back to the nursing school you and my mother attended so many years ago."

"But how? How did you know she was studying to become a nurse?"

"The people who found my mother wandering the streets of New York City remembered where they found her, and they remembered she wore a chain with the emblem of medicine dangling from it."

With great force, I instantly recall the day I refused the chain from Ella and how angry I was with her for deserting me. "I vividly remember your mother wearing that chain."

"From there, I was able to contact the nearby hospitals and nursing schools and asked if they had a record of any past workers or students whose first names were Nora. I spent a lot of time writing letters, but eventually, a very helpful administrator recalled yours and my mother's story from many years ago."

"But why didn't your mother tell you these things?"

"Sadly, my mother died while bringing me into this world, and the only thing she would utter until her death was your name. They say she did not have a strong will to live, which I've always felt all these years to be my fault."

"I can tell you right now, what happened to your mother could never be considered your fault. And I would say you are the brightest thing to have come from her life."

"That is very kind of you to say. I think it means so much to me after so many years of not knowing why my mother did not want to share her life with me."

Just as I am about to reveal everything to Ella's daughter, I notice a soft look in her eyes while she stares over my shoulder. As I turn to see Teodor standing in the doorway, I now see his eyes looking past me.

The room now silent, I imagine a place where words are left unsaid and hearts rejoice. But just as quickly, I realize I am glad to be here at this very moment, and I am so happy to be home.

# *Afterword*

Nora Emelia Anderson, was born January 15, 1881, in Rock Dell, Minnesota. She was the daughter of Nels K. and Elisa (Thorsen) Anderson. She attended Concordia College, Moorhead, Minnesota, and was a school teacher for ten years. She graduated from Deaconess Hospital, Grand Forks, North Dakota, as a trained nurse July 13, 1911. She entered service of the U.S. February 18, 1918, as an army nurse. She served overseas in Base Hospital No. 68, A.E.F. She died in the service, January 16, 1919 and was buried at Marss-sur-Allier, France, January 17, 1919. Her body was later moved to St. Mihiel American Cemetery, Thiaucourt, Meurthe-et-Moselle, France. In the U.S. Government records of this cemetery, her grave is listed as "Grave No. 30, Row 11, Block A."

Other than a few faded photographs, sometimes only the sparsest of information is available to a writer when attempting to create the life of a character similar to that of someone from generations past. Relatives with intimate knowledge have since passed on, and letters have been either lost or destroyed.

I've allowed myself a great deal of dramatic license, while projecting my own voice back to the past, in order to create a character that may have been similar to my great-aunt Nora. There are numerous historical facts throughout the story that pertain to my great-aunt and to her immediate family. The story is constructed from a number of actual events as well, such as the cyclone in New Richmond and the paperboy strike in New York City. However, the only actual setting as it relates to the real Nora is her military service as a nurse in France during World War I. All of the places the character Nora lives and the characters she encounters are fictitious, with the exception of Leo Tolstoy and his daughter, Alexandra.

Life is not a simple journey, and I think my great-aunt would have agreed with this notion given the circumstances she found herself on her last days on earth. To see oneself through to the end of a war—the Great War, no less—only to be felled by a malady, seems like the cruelest of all ironies. But I believe it is through her faith in her Savior Jesus Christ that she was able to accept her fate and reward.

I insisted that in my story Nora survive her bout with the Spanish flu to explore the question 'what if the real Nora had survived?' and to give her a fighting chance to return to the home of her childhood, to re-experience those things the real Nora undoubtedly longed for while facing death: family and friends, hopes and dreams, the smell of homemade bread, and the taste of a strong cup of Norwegian *kaffe* while watching the sunrise over the snow-drifted prairies. It's through these things she and I share that I can say I've always known her.